DAUGHTER
OF
SECRETS

DENISE DAYE

Don't forget to sign up for our newsletter to get FREE romance novels. You can find the newsletter and more info about our books here:

https://www.timelesspapers.com/newsletter.html

Thank you!

CONTENTS

CHAPTER ONE

O livia let out a tired groan when her alarm blared to life. She stirred to the side, reaching for her blanket. The cold night had turned into a cold morning; she shivered slightly. As the alarm beeped, forcing her back to reality, she wiggled her cold toes and sighed. She just wanted five more minutes.

One of her socks was gone, no doubt dragged away by Mr. Right, her cat. The fluffy kitty always had a way of getting her attention, especially when she was asleep—sitting on her chest and purring in her face, or like this morning, clawing away at her sock until it fell off.

The alarm beeped, its sounds cutting through the silence, seeming to pitch higher with each passing second.

"I'm up!" Olivia grunted and, as if it had listened to her, the alarm went silent. Almost immediately, Mr. Right pounced on the bed and let out a soft meow. Olivia smiled, blinking away the last trace of sleep in her eyes.

"Good morning, Mr. Right," she cooed and reached out to stroke him, running her fingers through the dark stripes on his brown fur. The cat purred in appreciation, his tail twitching.

"Please tell me you had a better night than I did," she said with a sigh and wiggled her toes again. "And where is my sock?"

Mr. Right meowed and pranced off her, his tiny feet tapping the floor as he ran off. Olivia got off the bed and sauntered into the bathroom. The silence ringing through the small apartment was one of the things she hated, and, ironically, it almost reflected the world she lived in: the quiet greyness and almost lack of interest.

Another day was starting, one where everything would go just as it had always gone on the rest. Olivia stared at her reflection and frowned.

"New day, same old story." She exhaled deeply as she put her shoulder-length brown hair into a bun. Water dripped out of the faucet into the cracked porcelain sink while she brushed her teeth and once again stared at her reflection. She hated what she saw on some days, the woman in her mid-thirties, looking tired and sad. But there was that brightness in her face that came whenever she smiled. Her hazel-brown eyes would sparkle and her oval-shaped face with a small button nose would take on a charismatic cuteness. "You've got the most beautiful smile," her ex had always told her. But finding things to smile about lately was just as hard as, well, sleeping through a beeping alarm clock. How do you keep smiling when the only person you have is the one you're looking at in the mirror?

Olivia stepped into the shower. The few minutes she spent under the warm spray of water always calmed her and, at the same time, hit her with lingering thoughts she wished would stay hidden. She lathered up her body, letting the soft lavender fragrance fill the air. There was something almost romantic to the smell, she thought, but romance was far from her reality at the moment. There were days she'd stay under the shower, closing her eyes, picturing a man she loved tinkering in the kitchen, making breakfast, hollering to ask if she wanted toast with her eggs. But as soon as she opened her eyes, he'd be gone and she'd once again be alone.

She shook away the fantasy. It wasn't real, not anymore.

The room felt cold as she stepped out of the bathroom and into her small living room. It was nothing fancy but had a nice rustic farmhouse look to it with white furniture on hardwood floors, plenty of plants, and a comfortable couch. Mr. Right stood by the doorframe linking the room to the short corridor, as if waiting for her.

"You're a good kitty, Mr. Right." She smiled and walked into the bedroom to start getting dressed for work. She ran her hands through her damp hair and let the brown strands drop over her shoulders. Olivia was slender with long legs. She wasn't all that "endowed" in the chest region, and it'd been that way since she was a blooming teenager, but her hips curved out nicely and she recalled having been told by someone—maybe her useless ex—that she had a nice body.

She straightened out her work outfit—the black skirt suit she'd ironed earlier—and once again stood before the mirror, turning from side to side, looking for more age-related changes. None today—she sighed in relief. For a while, she'd tried wearing makeup every day to work like her immaculate-looking coworkers, but after a few weeks, she traded those forty minutes of extra mirror time into sleeping time.

Olivia straightened the collar of her shirt and patted down a crease on her skirt. She let her eyes wander to the locket on her drawer and stretched her hand out to let the silver necklace slide into her palm. The locket clicked as she pressed a thumb over it. Her gaze softened when the picture inside came into view. The picture was dull and brown, but clear enough to show the pretty couple staring into the camera with bright, happy smiles.

"I wish you guys were here." Her shoulders sagged as she lowered her eyes, her voice somber. It felt like forever since the day of the car accident. She could still feel the shock, even as she stood there, staring at the locket. The pain was still fresh, numbing. It had been a few years—but not long enough for her to forget that shock.

Olivia pressed the locket to her chest, her eyes closed. It was hard to shake off that feeling of emptiness and fear each time she thought about her parents, and each time she held that locket. Since their death, there'd been no one to call or run to when she felt alone. They'd been hit by a drunk driver on their way back home from a date night. Olivia had just left for college when the police showed up at her door—it was the worst day of her life. She was literally left with no one else. No aunts, cousins, no grandparents. Her father had grown up as an only child, and her mother, a first-generation immigrant from Romania, always insisted that there was nothing and no one left for her in Romania, so that was that. Olivia was now one of those people with no family. Sometimes it made her shiver, the thought that if she died today, she'd leave nothing and no one behind.

Olivia slipped the necklace around her neck and spent the next few minutes making breakfast while Mr. Right moved around the small living room. He started scratching the couch, which she stopped with a scolding, "Ah-ah, no."

A half hour later, she was out of the house, fiddling with her door lock, which had started to jam of late.

"I'll have to get this fixed," she told herself and walked out into the cold morning, her shoes clacking on the hard concrete floor as she walked over to her aged 1990 silver Honda SUV. It was scratched and still had that dent in the back from someone committing a hit-and-run on her in the grocery parking lot, but working as an accountant at the local hospital didn't leave room in her finances for a new car right now.

"It's a good job," she'd always tell herself, though it certainly could be better, like those hot-shot doctors she saw in the hallways on their way to their clinics. But she couldn't complain—it paid for her apartment, cat, food, and monthly student loan repayments. It also served as a good distraction and time-killer. Unlike most of her coworkers, Olivia never had anything going on over the weekends—no screaming kids or online dates—so those days were always long and torturous for her.

Olivia parked her car in the employee parking lot of Boston Medical Center and walked up to the main entrance's big glass doors. Her office was located in a side wing of the hospital, so this was the quickest way.

The security man glanced up at her, tilted his black cap, and nodded with a mumble.

"Good morning," she greeted him with a smile. He acknowledged it with another serious nod. Olivia kept the smile on her face as she walked up the steps to the hospital entrance. "A smile brightens up the dark like opening the curtains to let the sunshine in," her mother always said.

She was reaching for the wooden door that led to the elevators when suddenly the door swung wide open. It clipped her fingers and she winced as she pulled her hand out of the way.

"Sorry about that," the man rushing out quickly apologized when he saw her and went on his way without waiting for a response, ambling down the steps, his brown jacket flying. Her fingers felt numb for a few more seconds before the pain faded.

"No worries," she mumbled and went inside to the elevators. Her destination: the accounting department on the third floor. She peeked over her shoulder and stared at the wooden door behind her, hoping someone else would show up for this elevator ride. Olivia had given up on the idea of a romantic encounter at the hospital—the competition was too fierce—but what about a friend? Some young woman, new in town, in need of a friend. They could engage in a conversation, start a lasting friendship. You know, like they do in the movies.

The elevator dinged and the doors slid open. A nurse stepped out, her light blue scrubs complementing her smooth skin. Something about the nurse reminded Olivia of those models she'd seen on magazine covers—her eyes gleaming, her perfect crimson red lips. Behind her, still in the elevator was Austin, Olivia's coworker.

"Hey Austin." Olivia stepped into the elevator. Austin was ogling the nurse as she disappeared behind the wooden door.

"Hmm?" He looked at her after the elevator doors closed. "Oh, Olivia. Hi."

"Good morning," she said.

"Morning," Austin said as he pulled out his phone, flicking his finger across the screen.

The ride went on for what seemed forever, the humming of the elevator filling the silent space. *How was your night?* she wanted to ask, but the words failed. Everything about his posture screamed: *Please don't talk to me!*

As soon as they got to the third floor, she stepped out in front of Austin and walked down the hall, past several voices echoing around her. She spotted an elderly lady up ahead, pushing a cart with cleaning supplies. Olivia smiled. Mindy was the floor cleaner and Olivia had known her since she started working there two years ago. She was a bit plump and short, her hair white like tropical sand. Despite the lines around her eyes, her face still had a certain lightness to it. Her hands were big and rough. "That's what happens when you do the job of the little people," she'd said with a smile.

Olivia remembered that awkward first day at the office. She'd felt like she was in high school all over again—the shy new girl just hoping to make friends. She'd walked into an empty break room, and that was when she met Mindy, busy with a mop. Mindy had smiled at her and made a joke, something about how these people ate like pigs. Since that day, Mindy had become her only friend in the building. Spotting her now, Olivia went over to say hi.

"Good morning, Mindy," she smiled.

"Not yet," Mindy said, nodding at an overflowing trash can in the hallway, "but it will be once I start on this mess." It was hard to guess how old she was. Her voice had the vibrant ring of a much younger woman, but Olivia had helped Mindy lift heavy trash bags into the dumpsters behind the hospital too many times to let that energetic voice fool her. If she had to guess, Olivia would have said Mindy was in her late seventies.

"Come get me if those bags get too heavy again," Olivia said.

Mindy offered her a thankful smile. "You're too kind for your own good."

"I have some paperwork to tidy up, but come get me when you're ready."

Mindy nodded and went back to work, dipping her hand into the cart to pull out a bottle of disinfectant while Olivia stepped into the office.

The accounting department was a large space with cubicles built into it, each housing two desks. A wide window overlooked the parking lot outside the hospital. Olivia's desk was next to the window, which she appreciated; she liked staring out at the vehicles moving in and out of the hospital—at the ambulances, sometimes, when they zoomed off for an emergency—and the lush lawns and flowers planted around the grounds.

Clutching her bag, she walked to her desk, muttering greetings each time she passed a coworker typing behind a computer. The office space housed just six people—four men and two women—who were all too busy to notice Olivia. When she reached her empty, tidy desk, she pushed back her chair and settled in, booting up her computer as she did.

Her cubicle mate was a middle-aged, short, toad-like guy named Darryl. He was still living with his mother, and Olivia had overheard her other coworkers joke that he had that serial killer look to him. Bald, pointy mustache, small eyes hiding behind taped glasses, always wearing the same worn brown pants with a pink striped shirt.

Darryl looked up when Olivia got to her desk. She smiled at him. He was an okay guy when he wanted to be.

"You came in early," Olivia said, and he shrugged.

"I'm always early."

These tiny chit-chats were the most Olivia ever got out of Darryl. He was more of a quiet guy, and Olivia had given up fishing for more.

The hours ticked by slowly as she worked, moving her mouse and staring at numbers and sighing intermittently. The hospital had lost a fair number of doctors to better-paying gigs last month, and those positions had now been filled with temporary physicians who were all on different salaries. It was a payroll nightmare, one that would take a while to correct.

"Hey Darryl," she called out softly. He kept his eyes focused on his computer, chewing loudly on a doughnut.

"Darryl," she repeated louder, and he grudgingly looked up.

"What?" He sounded annoyed.

"Just wanted to ask for your help with something."

"I'm busy," he replied and focused back on his computer.

Olivia frowned, but she was used to this by now. "Okay, sure. Later then."

When Olivia left the office for lunch, a tuna sandwich in her hand, she spotted Mindy again. The woman was bent over the floor, dipping a brush into a bucket of foamy water and sliding it over the tiles. Olivia decided to stop and talk for a few minutes; she needed it.

"Pretty busy today," Olivia joked as she leaned against the wall close to Mindy. Like most days, the hall was empty. Accounting was the last office on the third floor—the dead-end of the hospital.

Mindy looked up, a strand of her grey hair peeking out of the net around her head.

"I could hear a mouse's fart," Mindy said. "Or maybe that was Darryl." They both laughed. Mindy pressed down on the mop again. "Always working, but without much to show for it."

"I know that feeling," Olivia agreed, taking a bite of her sandwich. "I mean, here I am, working almost all day, and I can't shake off this feeling that something's missing."

Mindy arched an eyebrow, pausing in the slow back-and-forth brushing motion she'd been so intent on.

"I know what's missing in your life. Children." Mindy nodded.

Olivia smiled. "Well, for that I'd need a man first."

"Yeah, I guess there's the problem. Men these days aren't what they used to be. You better listen to an old woman who has been around a day or two."

"You're not *that* old, Mindy." Olivia looked down at the glistening surface of the tiles Mindy had mopped. Dried-up brown stains were splashed out on the white squares around the tiles.

Mindy scoffed. "Maybe not, but I'm old enough to know a swine from a mustang."

Suddenly Darryl stepped into the hallway, his hand down the back of his pants. He was scratching his butt without even bothering to see if anyone was around to witness. Mindy shook her head. "Not a mustang."

Mindy resumed mopping, her knuckles tight as she scrubbed hard on the stains.

"You know what I dream about, Olivia?"

"No, tell me."

Mindy stopped again and straightened her spine. "I just want to work for some rich family, who pays the big bucks, you know? Imagine working in a manor, fifty bucks an hour," she said, staring at the stains on the floor as if the more intensely she stared, the quicker her dream would become a reality.

"Well, wouldn't it be better to just dream of being rich?" Olivia wondered with a smile. Mindy shook her head.

"And sit on my ass all day waiting to die? Nah. I hope I'm working the day the Lord calls me."

Olivia stared at Mindy in admiration. She was as true as they came. "I'm sure your dreams will come true." She sounded even more certain than she had ever been about her own dreams.

That familiar beep sounded from her wristwatch. Lunch was over. Time always flew chatting with Mindy! She said bye and turned around before Mindy could ask her what her dreams were. She didn't want to be emotionally draining. Besides, no amount of money in the world could make her dreams come true.

***

It was already getting dark when Olivia parked in her usual spot in front of her apartment building. The cream-colored building looked grey beneath the thick, dark clouds hanging overhead. The evening was cool and windy, and it looked like it would rain tonight. On her way up the stairs to the second floor, she sighed when she remembered how difficult it was now to get into her apartment. She had already put in three work orders with the manager—all unanswered.

Biting her lip, she wiggled her hand and forced the key in the lock. Her face contorted when she tried turning it, wary of breaking the key and getting stuck outside in the cold. The key finally turned with a click and she pushed the door open.

"I'm home," she called out for Mr. Right and closed the door behind her. Mr. Right appeared from the kitchen, answering her with a little meow-purr combo. She smiled and leaned over to scratch his chin.

Olivia took off her black work shoes and coat and walked into the bedroom to change into her comfy clothes—grey sweats and matching sweater.

Followed by Mr. Right, she let herself fall onto her comfy couch. The evening was quiet as usual, so she picked up her phone and thought about texting her college friend Janice. After years of no contact, she'd encountered her at the supermarket a few months ago, and they'd exchanged numbers. Janice had never tried reaching out, and the few times Olivia tried calling, she'd always had to explain who she was.

"Could be worth a shot," she said to Mr. Right and typed a quick text, asking if Janice wanted to hang out. "Fingers crossed." The cat meowed and followed her as she went into the kitchen to make herself a frozen pizza.

As she was opening the freezer, Olivia's phone buzzed.

Sorry love, I can't. I'm a bit sick, gotta rest. Doc's orders. Maybe next time ☺

Olivia stared at her phone and read the text a few more times, but she'd been expecting this sort of response. Janice had always blown her off with some kind of excuse.

Propping up on the sofa, she turned on the TV and idly scrolled through her phone. She went through the routine: She did a quick run through her Facebook profile, checking for messages, which were never there; then she read her emails, which were mostly spam or work-related. She spotted an update from Janice on her Facebook page and sat up.

"Four minutes ago," she muttered under her breath. "Do you see that, Mr. Right?" she turned the phone to her cat, the backlight bright on his furry face. "She tells me she's sick but here she is." She paused and squinted to read the caption, "'Happy hour! Out with the girls.'" The photo was of a typical bar scene—dressed-up people squeezing together for the selfie, grinning wide, hands raised with colorful cocktails in them. Knowing Janice, she would be clubbing and drinking all night. Olivia tried to picture herself in a scene like that, with the skimpy dresses and alcohol and loud music. Partying wasn't her thing, to be honest—but then, she did enjoy watching the others dancing in a crowd. To her, the sight just screamed, "Life!"

She let out a sigh as Mr. Right dropped onto her thighs, settling down for some stroking. She tossed the phone on the sofa and picked up the remote, folding her legs in to give Mr. Right more space. She put on a comedy show and kept her eyes fixed on the flashing images. At times like this, her mind would stray to something else from her past—old memories she wished to suffocate. She thought about her last relationship—her best years wasted on a pig. She'd met Brandon at a Halloween party; they hit it off right away. Their relationship had lasted through her twenties, but, in the end, she'd had no choice but to end it. Olivia grabbed a throw pillow and squeezed it. She remembered the painful conversation as if it were yesterday.

"I was drunk. It just happened, you know. I got carried away," Brandon had said. "It wouldn't have happened if you'd come to the club with me."

"So it's my fault you slept with your ex?" she'd asked, going all hysterical. "Three times!"

"No, but you have changed, you know," he paused and frowned at her. "You're not as fun as you used to be, Olivia. You don't even like partying anymore."

"That's because I grew up, wanted to start a family," she'd cried out of frustration. Then he had the audacity to suggest that they could still do all that in a few years once he got a bit more fun out of his life—he was almost forty. She moved out the next day. He was never man enough to apologize to her and actually mean it.

"Gosh, I can't believe I cried for that guy," Olivia said, trying hard to focus on the movie. Years of her life, gone. She always seemed to land in relationships where she'd get cheated on, and, most times, during the pain and heartbreak, she'd tell herself that it was all her fault for not acknowledging the red flags sooner. But the guys were so darn good at hiding them, and she always seemed to see the best in people— a great quality for a social worker but not for a thirty-something woman trying to find a decent man. Why could people not see through her quiet, calm nature to who she truly was: not boring, but loyal. Not naïve, but kind-hearted. Not stuck-up, but hard-working. Not clingy, but loving and devoted. It seemed that people these days were judged by their ability to drink and crack jokes—that was it.

She wasn't sure how long the movie stayed on, but, hours later, when she slowly opened her eyes to the flashing lights from the TV, she yawned, turned it off, and went to her bedroom. A new day always brought with it hope. And besides, there was no better place to indulge in her fantasies than in her dreams.

***

The next morning, Olivia went to work. She might as well have been dropped into a loop, where everything played back as it had the day before. The doctors in the entrance hall barely glanced at her as she passed; their interested gazes were reserved for the pretty girls. Then she said hello to Mindy as always and went into the office.

Shortly after settling in at her desk, Mike, her supervisor, stopped by, which was odd in every way, given that he never dropped by to see anyone. The tall, older man had a curious look in his grey eyes as he said, almost in a hushed voice, "Do you have a minute, Olivia? It's important."

Olivia's eyes widened and the man smiled, his smooth, bald head glistening. "Don't worry, nothing to panic over."

Olivia scoffed. "I'm glad I'm not fired."

"Oh, no. You aren't," Mike said.

Olivia nodded and followed him into his office. A man was sitting on one of the white plastic chairs behind a big wooden desk, upon which sat a computer, several piles of paperwork, and a framed picture of Mike, his wife, and their two grown daughters, all dressed in ugly Christmas sweaters and smiling for the camera. The office was small but had its own window. *The comfort of a supervisor,* Olivia thought.

"This is Mr. Stanley." Mike introduced her as the short, stocky, well-dressed man stood up. He had dark hair, which seemed dyed, and a trimmed moustache over his lips. There was an important air around him, so when Mike added that the man was a lawyer, Olivia wasn't entirely surprised. He looked like one. His immaculate suit and confident grin screamed *lawyer*.

Mr. Stanley rose from his seat and stretched his hand out for a handshake. Olivia shook it, still trying to wrap her head around what was happening.

"I have some business to take care of," Mike said to her, all smiles like he knew something she didn't. He made his way toward the door. "Mr. Stanley here has to talk to you. I'm sure you'll be pleased."

Olivia nodded, confused, as Mike closed the door behind him.

"Miss Carter," the lawyer started as soon as they were alone. He smiled and adjusted his black suit jacket. "Why not take a seat?" he offered, gesturing to the other empty seat.

"I think I'm good," Olivia said. "Am I in some kind of trouble?"

The lawyer laughed, shaking his head as the rich, deep sound escaped his throat. "Quite the contrary, Miss Carter."

She caught a hint of a European accent in his voice. It sounded well-refined. British? The lawyer lifted a finger to his moustache, running it along the length of the left side, then the right.

"I must apologize for showing up here unannounced." He paused, smiled, and reached for a folder sitting on the desk. "But I would like to get straight to the point if that is agreeable with you?" He handed her the folder. Olivia took it, balancing it in her hands as she flipped it open.

Inside, she found several photos and a few documents, all on white papers except for one photo—which was clipped to the folder—of an old man Olivia wasn't sure she recognized. He was wearing a suit and had a tall, slender stature. A good-looking man, Olivia thought, even for his age.

"Are you sure you don't want to take a seat?" Mr. Stanley asked again, but this time she didn't respond. She scanned the file slowly, the expression on her face folding into a perplexed frown.

"This man in the picture"—Mr. Stanley pointed his long finger at it—"that's your mother's first husband, Andrei Rusu."

Olivia glanced up. "Wait, what? My mother's what?"

"First husband," he repeated unemotionally. "You were not aware that she was married before?"

Olivia slowly shook her head. "I've never . . .She's never mentioned him before. But my mom never spoke much of her life in Romania before she came here. She didn't like to be reminded of it."

He nodded. "Andrei Rusu was Romanian, just like your mother."

The fact that her mom had been married before was shocking, but not *that* shocking. Her mom was allowed to have a life before she met her dad. And yet, it had always bothered Olivia that she knew so little of her Romanian origins. She focused on the picture again, taking in the features of this Andrei Rusu. His focused eyes matched his brown hair, which had a few silver strands that fell over his lean, handsome face.

"There's more," Mr. Stanley said. Olivia shifted her gaze back to him. He smiled when she grabbed the white plastic chair and settled into it.

"I think what you are about to hear next is a little more shocking," he said, a calmness in his tone that Olivia didn't share. What was going on here?

"Andrei Rusu is the owner of the Rusu fast-food chain. You have heard of it, I suppose?"

Olivia straightened and blinked rapidly. "The Rusu fast-food chain?" The cogs in her head turned. Rusu? Slowly the images formed, pictures flashing in her mind. "Yes, I've heard of it. They're big in Europe and recently opened a few restaurants here as well."

"Quite right. Rusu Corporation is rather large. A multi-billion-dollar industry, to be exact." Mr. Stanley had a satisfied smile on his face. "I've had the pleasure of being Andrei Rusu's personal lawyer for almost all his life." Olivia looked at him in confusion. He cleared his throat. "Anyway, to get to the point, Andrei Rusu has recently passed away and named you his heir to his estate, including the Rusu cooperation, all personal assets, and his real estate."

Olivia's mouth fell open. Mr. Stanley was still rambling on. "Well some of the real estate is rather outdated, the castles at least, but there is a nice mansion just outside of town that he occupied whenever—"

"I am *what*?!" Olivia interrupted him, realizing too late that she had yelled. The folder shook in her trembling hands. Mr. Stanley gave her a moment.

"Yes, of course, this must be rather unexpected for you. My apologies. Let me repeat that once more. You are the sole heir to the Rusu fortune."

Olivia leaned back in her seat. Her lips moved, but no words came out. Her hands were still trembling as her fingers turned white from her grip on the folder.

"A m-mistake," she said, her voice foreign to her.

"Oh, there's no mistake. Andrei has been very clear about this, both through my own personal conversations with him as well as in his notarized will."

Olivia shook her head, mouth still wide open. "A-a joke then? Hidden camera?" She scanned the office for a camera crew. This was ridiculous. A secret first husband and a Romanian billionaire leaving her everything? Come on!

Mr. Stanley analyzed her, then sighed. "Let me clarify further."

She nodded, her head moving in slow motion.

"Andrei Rusu loved your mother very much," Mr. Stanley explained. "To him, it was one of those once-in-a-lifetime sort of things, you see. He never loved again after your mother, and he spoke of her often, even to me. He had no children, so there has always been the issue of his vast fortune and who would inherit it. That's where you come in; he chose you, the child of his only true love, to inherit it all."

Olivia crossed her arms in front of her. "Just like that?"

"Just like that."

"Mm-hmm. Millions of dollars just like that, huh? To his old love's only child?" She raised her eyebrows.

"No. Not millions. His estate is worth well over a billion. But yes, to his love's only child."

"So there was no one else? Didn't he have any other relatives? He didn't even know me."

Mr. Stanley shrugged. "This has nothing to do with what you or I think, only what is legal in the eyes of the law. Although—" He paused and straightened his tie. Olivia narrowed her eyes at him. *Here we go.*

"Although what?"

"Andrei Rusu does have a sister and a niece in Romania."

"And they're alive?" Olivia asked.

"Very much so, yes. But they didn't inherit anything. Everything went to you."

Olivia frowned. "Why?"

Mr. Stanley shrugged once more but this time he seemed uneasy. "Something about an argument, but Andrei never spoke much of them to me and he didn't pay me to stick my nose in matters he wanted to keep to himself. In the eyes of the law, remember?" He leaned back in his chair. "He could have left it to the homeless if it pleased him. It was his money." Mr. Stanley cleared his throat. "Well, anyway, I need a few signatures from you so we can start the whole process. You don't mind, do you?"

Olivia stared at him in dead silence, the mixture of shock, disbelief, and skepticism paralyzing her. She was to be the sole heiress of the Rusu food corporation? Her? Olivia Carter, the quiet, lonely accountant from Boston that most would describe as boring?

"Good, I'm glad you don't mind," Mr. Stanley rumbled, putting a pen into her limp hand. "Now sign here, here, there, here, there, here, here, here, aaaaand here too."

CHAPTER TWO

L ife turned upside down for Olivia in the days that followed. It was nothing short of thrilling! She was rich beyond belief. A dream had become true! But then there was also this feeling as if a heavy weight had suddenly, and mercilessly, been dropped on her. Except, this weight came with enormous wealth. It took her a while to really start believing that Mr. Stanley was telling the truth. She was always on the lookout for that hidden camera crew, but with the new bank accounts, the corporate meetings, the luxury cars, and, finally, the pair of golden keys to the Boston Rusu mansion, she had become a believer. An utterly shocked—and a bit terrified—believer.

That mansion sat at the edge of town in a filthy-rich neighborhood. It stretched out on a wide estate surrounded by green fields and woods. When Olivia stepped out of the chauffeur-driven black Rolls Royce, she practically shook with wonder. The view was perfect, the way the blue sky stretched over the red brick façade of the colossal manor, blending with golden rays of sunshine. It was all a dream.

"I should have brought my camera," she mumbled at the chauffeur, who smiled professionally at her.

Mr. Stanley got out of his black Mercedes and walked around the other side of the car to stand beside Olivia. "His favorite of all his residences. Andrei spent most of his final years here," he said.

Olivia clasped her hands in front of her face and stared at the mansion. A huge fountain sat in the middle of the large grounds, forming two majestic stallions with jets of water springing in circles around them. The grounds had a beautifully crafted array of flowers lining the manicured green lawns. From the exotically colored petals, Olivia wasn't sure she'd ever seen these kinds of flowers before.

"This . . . is . . . beautiful!" Olivia moved toward the mansion. Two gardeners stood by the flowers as she walked past. They bowed respectfully, and Olivia, in reflex, bowed back. While she admired the flowers and the beautiful fragrance in the air, she half-expected to hear a snap as this new world peeled away, like a rug drawn from under her feet; she expected her grey reality to rush back and remind her that this was all a dream. Yet, the birds fluttering overhead, the cool breeze, and the people standing around her all seemed real, as real as she did, as real as this inheritance seemed to be.

"How come Andrei never tried to contact my mom again? If he loved her so much?" Olivia wondered as they climbed up the steps and stopped in front of a white-gloved butler, his hand on a golden door handle, ready to open the entrance to the mansion.

"Wasn't your mother married to your father?" Mr. Stanley answered her question with his own.

Olivia frowned. "Well, yeah."

"Andrei was a man of character. It wouldn't have been his style to cause drama. Now, would you like to tour your new home? It's rather impressive."

Olivia found herself nodding enthusiastically. "I've never been one to be impressed by material things," she muttered to herself as she stepped into the breathtaking entrance hall. It had herringbone hardwood floors and ceilings as high as a small church. Large landscape paintings decorated the walnut-paneled walls. A colossal, round chandelier with candlelight bulbs was hanging from the wooden ceiling.

"This is beautiful," she gaped. "I can't believe people live in mansions like this."

"Of course people still live in mansions," Mr. Stanley said with a chuckle. "But only a very few lucky ones, I suppose."

Without emotion, the butler opened the large doors to the formal living room—one of many, she guessed. Her mouth dropped once again.

Red carpet, lush and soft, stretched over the formal living room. There were wide windows inside wooden arches reaching almost to the ceiling, the glass gleaming with sunlight. Deep red curtains hung beside them. Olivia craned her neck as she gazed at the golden silk furniture placed strategically around a crackling fire in an enormous stone fireplace that reminded her of a medieval castle. Several smaller crystal chandeliers brightened the room, shimmering like diamonds.

"This way," Mr. Stanley beckoned, and Olivia nodded.

They came to a large staircase. The steps, covered with gold-lined red carpet, formed a half-circle, leading to the second floor. The walls on the staircase were covered with beautiful paintings and portraits of people Olivia didn't recognize.

"Andrei . . . I mean Mr. Rusu lived here alone? No family?" Olivia wondered.

"That's right."

"It's such a huge place."

Mr. Stanley smiled as they turned onto the second floor's hallway. Olivia pointed at the shields mounted on the wall then let her gaze wander to the swords, maces, and medieval armor on a full figure of a knight, still and imposing.

"Are these real? I mean . . . original?" she asked.

"Everything in this mansion is original," Mr. Stanley answered with a cocky grin forming on his face. "Andrei was something of a collector, you see. Medieval armor, weaponry, and things like that, especially from Romania. Most of the items you see here are from his castles in Romania, family heirlooms," he said matter-of-factly.

"I thought Andrei Rusu was self-made?" Olivia asked, peeking over her shoulder at the knight she'd just passed.

"He was. His family lineage stems from impoverished Romanian aristocracy. He climbed his way back up, so to speak," Mr. Stanley said.

She frowned. All of this was so bizarre, especially the fact that this was all hers now.

"Is something wrong, Olivia?" Mr. Stanley asked.

"No, not really. I'm still trying to make sure this isn't a dream. I mean, not that long ago I was a boring accountant, a lonely cat lady from Boston. Now I'm Olivia Carter, silent owner of Rusu Corporations, filthy rich and owner of castles and swords and shields? I don't want to seem ungrateful, but it feels so . . . strange."

She stopped at a huge painting of a thin man with fierce eyes and a confident smile. One hand was in his left pocket while the other rested flat against his chest, his fingers sporting golden rings with what looked like green crystals.

"Is that him?"

Mr. Stanley nodded. "Andrei Rusu. He truly was a great man."

"And he loved my mother," Olivia muttered to herself, the whole idea still astounding her to the core. There were so many questions she wished she could ask, but her mother was dead, and whenever she asked him about personal matters, Mr. Stanley always gave her the same old, "I don't know. I was just his lawyer."

"And you said he has a sister, in Romania?"

"Yes, Elena Rusu."

"Why did he leave nothing to her? He had so much."

Mr. Stanley shrugged. She knew his answer, so she beat him to it: "You don't know, you were just his lawyer."

Mr. Stanley laughed. "Quite right, but they didn't seem to have a relationship with one another. But don't ask me why . . . I was just his lawyer." He grinned, and this time Olivia did too.

"Come now, we still have to finish this tour, and I have a meeting this afternoon."

She nodded. "Yes, thank you for showing me around. I know this goes beyond your duty."

Despite all the questions on her mind, she was more than thankful to Mr. Stanley for being her tour guide and accompanying her to important meetings, such as the "Rusu Corp New Owner Meet and Greet." Although Olivia wasn't involved in the business aspect of the Rusu Cooperation, she still was the silent majority shareholder and, as such, had to attend a few meetings. Boy, were those awkward. Olivia had sat in a large leather chair at the end of a long mahogany table in the conference room at the Rusu cooperation headquarters while a bunch of old, important-looking men in suits stared at her, their eyes intense and unwelcoming as if wondering if this was a joke. Without Mr. Stanley by her side, she would have melted into that seat like a popsicle in a microwave

Moving into this mansion was just one of the many things that changed in Olivia's life, and all of it was jarring. At first, she was ecstatic and danced and jumped around her tiny living room, Mr. Right tightly squeezed in her arms. But then, after actually living there for a few days, wandering through all those empty rooms, it made her feel even more lonely than she was before.

A soft vibration woke her from a deep Sunday-morning slumber. Her eyes slowly opened to find the same scene she had for the last few days: cream silken sheets on a king-sized bed, a spacious bedroom with luxurious, white furniture, and the burnt-down charcoal from last night's wood in her stone fireplace.

"Look, Mr. Right," Olivia said to her tubby cat, who was sleeping by her feet on a red cashmere blanket, purring like a king who had finally come home to his palace. "We're still here; it's not a dream."

Olivia grabbed her phone from the wooden nightstand and glanced at it. A missed call from an unknown number.

"My phone never rings in the morning. In fact," she said, staring at the number, "it never rings at all."

Mr. Right ignored her, closing his eyes and purring even louder. She couldn't help but grin. Cats truly were divas.

A worry crept into Olivia's mind. She had taken off from work for two weeks. She'd had so much unused vacation time, she could have flown to the moon and back. Was something the matter? Did they fire her thinking she didn't need the job any longer? It was ridiculous to be anxious about an accounting job with all the money she had now, especially considering the pressure from Mr. Stanley to quit, as it was "unfitting, in view of her new circumstances." But what would she do all day without a job? She'd worked her whole life, just like her mother and father. A loaded bank account wouldn't change those values overnight.

With a pounding heart, she called back the missed call. It rang only one time before a woman shouted "Olivia!" in an energetic, high-pitched voice. The tone was so sharp and unexpected that Olivia jerked her head away from the phone.

"How wonderful! This is so cool!" The woman's voice was so enthusiastic, her words rolled off her tongue almost too quick for Olivia to grasp.

"I'm sorry, I'm not sure who I'm speaking with," Olivia said.

"Silly! It's Elizabeth. You know, from work," she replied, and the voice began to sound familiar. But Olivia had never taken a call with Elizabeth . . . in fact, the last memory she had of Elizabeth was when Elizabeth and another coworker had been talking about a Halloween party, but had grown quiet the moment they saw Olivia.

"Yes, Elizabeth."

"Yeah, from work." Elizabeth hesitated for a moment before asking, "How have you been?"

Olivia frowned. It felt strange hearing that question from a colleague who never spoke to her; and after the whole Halloween party thing, it felt almost deceitful and insulting.

"So . . . I heard what happened, Olivia. Incredible. Amazing! It must be exciting?"

Olivia sighed and pressed her hand on the bed, marveling once more at how extra soft the silk was. It felt like sleeping on clouds.

Elizabeth mercilessly went on, ignoring Olivia's silence. "I even saw you on national TV when you came out of that big shiny skyscraper. Wow! And you looked so damn gorgeous and important with that sleek lawyer by your side. So how much money—"

"Um, can I call you back?" Olivia cut in and ended the call before getting a response.

National TV? She'd thought those cameras when she came out of the Rusu Corp meeting were maybe a local, short clip at the most.

She pulled away the folds of the warm blanket, searching for the remote. Last night she'd binge-watched thrillers on the large TV in her room. Mr. Right had been by her side, like he always was, except this time they were in a huge room with bedding capable of swallowing someone, and a mansion with halls so grand she needed a map to navigate them.

The TV, wide as it was, stretched out from the ceiling like a recliner. It was amazing.

She found the remote and skipped through the major TV channels, all the while shaking her head over the call she'd just received. "So she knows I'm her colleague now, huh?"

Olivia was about to turn the TV off again when she saw her face on a news report. Her heart skipped a beat as the gigantic image of herself flashed brightly in front of her.

BOSTON WOMAN INHERITS BILLION-DOLLAR RUSU FORTUNE

She stared at the screen, her heart thumping fast, her hands trembling. Millions of people would be watching this right now. Her face would be all over the country. The room spun around her. She stumbled out of the bed and tore one of the doors in the room wide open.

"Damn, a closet!" she groaned and took a few steps back and repeated her motions with the door next to that one, which thankfully turned out to be the bathroom. She rushed in and leaned over the sink. Her knuckles were white as she held on to the bowl, staring at her reflection, the high-end white marble bathroom with golden finishes felt somehow threatening.

The caption was still in her head, the words flashing before her. She turned on the faucet, her eyes blurring again as the water rushed into the sink. Placing her hand under the water, she let the cold splash against her skin like an intense wake-up call. This was no dream. She splashed some of the water on her face and blinked away a few drops, exhaling slowly.

It'll be over soon. It's just routine news coverage. Pretty sure the world has more important things to talk about than Olivia Carter, rich or not.

Suddenly her phone vibrated again. Olivia rushed back into her bedroom and caught it just in time.

"Hello?"

"Olivia, hey, it's Janice."

Ah, yes, her flaky friend, always-sick Janice.

"Oh, Janice. I thought you'd forgotten me because you never returned my last text. Or the one before that."

An awkward chuckle came from the other end. "No, I was sick, remember?"

"Okay," Olivia answered.

"So, Olivia, I heard about, um, you know . . . Wow, the Rusu fortune! That's crazy. We have to celebrate."

She sounded excited, but that fake, thin-layered excitement one portrayed when trying to get something from someone else. Mr. Right purred and twitched his whiskers, glancing up at Olivia as if telling her to hang up.

"Oh yeah, that," she answered casually. "Pretty crazy times we live in."

"True that. Anyways, me and the girls were wondering if you wanted to hang soon? Maybe at your mansion? I realized we haven't really hung out in so long. Especially since I've been, you know, sick."

"You're right," she answered and smiled when she heard a quick intake of breath. "But . . ."

"But?" Janice asked, exhaling on the other end.

"But you see, Janice, I'm quite busy these days. I'll take a rain check on that and get back to you. Like you said you would, pretty much every time I called."

Before Janice could mutter anything else, Olivia ended the call and sighed deeply.

"Hang out at my place? Yeah right." She got up and walked to her closet, pressing her feet into the lush carpeting and enjoying the softness caressing her feet, a feeling she was sure she would never get tired of.

She opened the closet door and walked in. It was like a hall on its own. It was almost funny how the wide space was empty except for the few items she'd brought along. Her gaze wandered to the worn blue wool sweater Mindy had gotten her for Christmas last year. She had worn it so often, it came apart at the bottom. Maybe it was time to go shopping. After all, was that not what tons and tons of money was for?

She ran her hand over the rough blue wool and along one of the threads that had become loose.

"You know what?"

Mr. Right meowed in response.

"I should offer Mindy a job. She's always dreamed of working in a place like this. I'm sure we now count as rich people, don't you think?"

Mr. Right stretched out on the bed. Olivia got dressed in jeans and her favorite blue sweater and headed downstairs to ask the driver to drop her off downtown.

But what was supposed to be a fun day at the mall, like the shopping scene in *Pretty Woman*, turned out to be one of the most annoying days of her life. Every minute was filled with buzzing phone calls and texts and constant disturbances. It was unbearable. She received phone calls from people she went to high school with and even all the way back from kindergarten. How did all these people get her number anyway?

Of course, her pig ex was the frontrunner of the text harassments, talking about how she was always his true love and asking if they could talk.

At some point, Olivia decided to turn the phone off. She was at a shoe store looking at cute leather boots, without having to check the price tag for the first time in her life, when Olivia decided enough was enough and put an end to the show. It was not like she would miss an important call, and this sudden interest in her—no, not her, her money—made her sad more than it annoyed her. Did these people have no dignity at all? Think her an idiot?

She was on her way to the register, boots in hand, when for the first time she wondered if Mr. Stanley was right about quitting her job. Would it be as bad at the office as it was with all these calls and texts? But then, she loved to go to work. Not the job per se, but the part where she was out of the house, killing time. Work gave her purpose. Olivia sighed. There were only six other people in her immediate department. How bad could it be?

***

Olivia went back to work the next week—a tricky task, given the now-constant "plastic" attention everyone was giving her. She couldn't walk down a hall, or into an elevator, without everyone trying to act all nice and interested in her all of a sudden. It was crazy, and it weighed her down. She'd walk into the hospital quietly, as she'd always done, but now the handsome doctors at the entrance hall smiled at her and greeted her—some even asked her out. This would have been a dream if it'd happened before her story had spread, but, sadly, she knew what all the sudden interest was about—her bank account, not her.

Then there were the unbearable, non-stop visits from her coworkers. "Just checking in to see how you're doing," they'd say, wondering if she would "like to hang out." Elizabeth was leading the charge, even telling employees from other floors to leave her alone, rolling her eyes at them, totally oblivious to the fact that she was just like them—maybe even worse. Only Darren didn't seem to care about her sudden fame and fortune, staring at his computer like he always did, his googly eyes reflecting the lights of the monitor like a mirror.

Nights at the mansion still reminded her of the nights she'd spent at her old apartment—just that they felt even lonelier. All she saw was huge, empty space.

The dining hall was a medieval-like room with a huge fireplace. Its soft yellow and orange flames threw a comfortable light onto the long table, which was set with a fancy candelabra in the center and priceless porcelain china hundreds of years old.

Like most days, she sat alone at this long table, silence ringing through the air, occasionally punctuated by the clanking of cutlery on her plate and the footsteps of a woman called Johanna, one of the maids of the house. Olivia had decided to keep all staff in the mansion. There was no point making them lose their jobs, although it felt ridiculous that someone did all her cooking and laundry. There was also the issue of how colossal and intimidating the mansion was; it was nice seeing people around now and then.

Johanna, a middle-aged and well-fed woman, approached her politely and cleared up the plates.

"Thank you, thank you so much for your help," Olivia said, watching in embarrassment as Johanna cleaned up after her. She had tried to help before, but Johanna would refuse her help quite strongly. Johanna was about to turn and leave, but Olivia cleared her throat.

"Johanna, what was Andrei Rusu like?" she asked.

Johanna looked up at her and smiled. "I don't know much about him, Miss Carter."

"You can call me Olivia."

Johanna gave her a polite smile. "Yes, Miss Carter. I know he was a very lonely man. He worked all the time, always serious, but he treated us well. I think he had a sister in Romania. But we never heard him talk to her, no. Never even mentioned her. I heard his lawyer talk about her with him once."

"Hmm. I wonder why," Olivia mumbled.

"I don't know, I'm sorry," Johanna muttered with another smile, then twirled around and left the dining hall.

Why wouldn't he talk to his only sister? Olivia took a sip of her wine.

"Gosh, it's really buzzing in here," Mindy's voice echoed through the dining hall. Olivia smiled and turned to the wide-open French double door. It was always good to see a friendly face. Olivia had hired Mindy and placed her on a salary equivalent to that of a hedge fund manager. She even told Mindy that she could just take the money and retire, but Mindy had gotten mad, growling something about not being a charity case and that she works for her money—especially *that* much. Sometimes Olivia wondered if she was more or less paying her for being her only friend for the last few years, as absurd as it sounded.

"You're here late, Mindy," Olivia said and Mindy nodded.

"I came in later and felt like pretending I had work to do, given how there's next to nothing to clean; the other full-time staff leave everything spotless."

"You're not going to start a cleaners' war or something, are you?" Olivia mused with a smile.

"The floors glisten like mirrors," Mindy responded with a mix of admiration and disappointment. "It makes the place look sterile."

She took a seat at the long wooden table next to Olivia and scanned the dining hall. Her silver hair was in a braid and glittering in the light of the fireplace.

"So, how has all this been? Must feel like a dream."

"A wild dream," Olivia added. "I've never imagined living in a place like this, but here we are." She sighed.

"You make it sound like it's a bad thing. Is something wrong?"

Olivia shifted her gaze to her fingers, scraping the nails together. "I . . . well, I don't want to seem ungrateful or anything, and I'm not, really." She paused and looked up. "But all this seems so . . . strange. It's nice and all, finding out that you weren't so alone in the world after all and that someone you've never met loved your mother enough to pass on their fortune to you, but the circumstances around it make me a bit uncomfortable."

"How so?" Mindy reached for one of the several empty glasses on the table and filled it with wine from the bottle in front of Olivia. The red liquid splashed into the glass. This wasn't the first time they'd shared a glass of wine together here. Olivia loved chatting over a glass or two, like good friends.

"Don't you find it strange that I got to keep everything—the money, the businesses, this lovely mansion—but she got nothing."

"Who?"

"Andrei's sister. She's somewhere in Romania, penniless from what I've heard. I mean, I never knew my mother had this secret wealthy first husband and now he has a sister who probably thinks—" Olivia broke off.

"That you stole the money doing God knows what."

Olivia nodded. "Exactly."

Mindy frowned. "It's a lot of money."

"It is."

"Have you considered . . ."

"Giving her some? Yes, I have. I feel like it'd be the right thing to do. I don't need all of this," Olivia said, stretching out both arms.

Mindy sat silently for a while, then looked up at Olivia. "You should go to Romania."

Olivia raised her head, her interest drawn. "What? Me?"

"Yes, you. Didn't you say your mother was from Romania?"

Olivia scratched her chin. "Yes, but I kinda was thinking about wiring her the money."

"Why? Go to Romania, find the sister, and give her some money in person. Who knows? Maybe you still have some family over there. Distant aunts, cousins. I have them all over the country; I've always wanted to go hunt them down just for fun."

Olivia turned it over in her head, and the more she thought about it, the more interesting and appealing the idea became. "My mom was pretty secretive about her past."

"There you go."

"And I did look for relatives on my father's side here in the U.S. There are literally none—expect for two cousins who never replied to my emails."

"Mm-hmm," Mindy mumbled. "Now it's time to do the same on your mother's side. In Romania."

Olivia tipped her head back, finishing her glass of wine in one, smooth motion. Then she shook her head with a smile.

"What?" Mindy wondered.

"Nothing. I was just thinking that this whole thing is getting crazier and crazier."

Mindy smiled. "You'll go then?"

Olivia smiled back at her then bit her lip.

Mindy raised her glass. "Now that is something to cheers to! Olivia Carter—kind-hearted heiress and adventurous world traveler."

Olivia refilled her glass and raised it with a huge grin. "I'll cheers to that." Their glasses clinked together. "Let's hope Andrei's sister is happy to see me."

CHAPTER THREE

Elena Rusu spat out the window, grimacing at the sight of grime and filth stretching through the narrow street of rundown old farmhouses. A middle-aged man passed by, completely unperturbed by the mucky water spilling onto the street from broken pipes or even the worn laundry flapping on the clothesline overhead. The man gazed at Elena, and she growled at him. He smiled politely and threw her a curt nod, then averted his gaze, hastening his steps.

Elena rolled her eyes and scoffed, shifting her gaze to a broken hand mirror resting on the windowsill.

"Cursed men," she grunted, frowning at the bags under her eyes and the lines forming on her skin. She sighed, knowing the days of her youth were far behind her now. She was thin and tall, but not as tall as her daughter, Alina, who was sitting on the worn orange couch behind her.

"I used to be pretty, you know," Elena said. "The kind of woman the Americans called dolls after the war." The word *doll* always rolled off her tongue with an accent. Elena had a pale complexion, which complemented both the fake black dot above her thin lips and her bright blue eyes. Her wrists were adorned with colorful bracelets, her thin fingers and neck overladen with fake rings and necklaces.

Looking around the small, old house she shared with Alina, she was unable to hold back another sigh, heavier than the last. Stained wallpaper was peeling off the walls, and the battered furniture and outdated appliances cluttered the rooms.

"We should be living better than this ... may he rot in hell," she muttered, her eyes moving from the cracked ceiling to the cobwebs in the corners as she listened to the scratching of what she was sure was a rat scampering behind the thin wooden walls.

Behind her, thick smoke rose through the air. She turned around and glared at Alina, who was clutching a thin cigarette in her long fingers with pink nail polish. She was beautiful, with striking grey eyes. Her hair was blonde; a few strands had fallen out of her bun and over the side of her face. She was dressed in tight pink jeans and a purple sweater, her heavy makeup spotless.

Elena looked back at the mirror and slammed it onto the windowsill with a grunt.

Alina looked up when she heard the smash. "Do you mind? I was going to use that later."

"You wouldn't have to use mine if you'd get yourself a man who can buy you your own things, huh, Alina?" Alina focused back on her phone, taking a short draw from the cigarette which had already been smoked down to the butt.

"You know I don't want to play wifey for an old man. I want to go to univ—"

"Dreams, dreams, nothing but dreams!" Elena barked.

Alina frowned. "What's going on with you today? You seem angrier than usual."

Elena grunted and placed her hands on her waist. Her eyes flashed when she saw the crumpled cigarette pack on the floor.

"Did you smoke the last cigarette again?" she said, her voice rising higher as it usually did whenever she got upset. Alina rolled her eyes and sat upright on the couch, brushing off the ash from her pink pants.

"Yeah, so?" Alina snapped back at her mother.

"You selfish dog!"

"I'll pay for the next pack," Alina muttered under her breath.

Elena fumed. "Oh yes, I forgot. With all those millions you make selling the farmer's produce at that dingy little market." She threw her hands in the air and paced around the room, looking for another pack of cigarettes. "Go do something useful and get yourself a man, a rich one. Maybe then we won't have to live in a place like this, like animals."

Alina finished her cigarette with a frown, pinched her nostrils, and puffed out the smoke, flicking the thing into an overflowing ashtray.

Elena grabbed the old, blackened kettle by the kitchen counter with the intention of making a strong coffee, but she set it back down. "I need a stiffer drink."

She fumbled around the mess on the kitchen counter, peering over her shoulder to make sure Alina wasn't watching while she reached for her secret stash of whisky. She grabbed a glass, blew out the dirt in it, taking a whiff and deciding there wasn't any need to rinse it out. She poured the drink and quickly hid the bottle, leaning back on the counter as she poured the burning liquid down her throat—not wincing once.

"To think my brother died and didn't leave us a penny."

"Not this again!" Alina shouted from the cramped living room.

Elena continued bemoaning. "Leaves it all to some stranger. Endless piles of money—gone." She stared at the remaining whisky in the glass and tightened her face, muttering through her teeth. "I knew Maria was nothing but trouble the first time Andrei laid eyes on her. Bewitched. That's what she did to him. Magic. Who in their right mind would leave all his money to some woman's daughter, not even his own? And what does he do to us, his real family? He casts us out!"

Elena felt a burning hot rage take over her body. She was about to throw the glass against the wall, when her eyes caught the corner of a white letter on the countertop, buried under a pile of old newspapers and bills. She stepped closer, staring at the white envelope, and caught the words *United States of America*. She frowned, then reached for the letter and slipped it out, not minding the other papers, which tumbled to the floor. She flipped the letter over in her hands and saw it was sent by an Olivia Carter.

OLIVIA CARTER!

With shaking hands, Elena snapped at her daughter, "How long has this been here?"

Alina looked up to see the letter Elena was waving around. "I don't know, a few weeks or so . . . maybe. What does it matter?"

"What does it—" She paused, inhaling deeply. "What does it matter?" she repeated, yelling. "Why didn't you tell me?"

Alina snorted and looked away without much interest. "Who's Olivia anyway?"

The thought of this letter sitting on the counter for weeks made Elena want to break something. She turned away from her daughter, unable to look at her. The paper crinkled as she tore open the envelope.

Elena heard Alina slide off the couch, moving over to the kitchen counter. Elena looked up and saw that whiny look on her daughter's face—one she got whenever she was scolded.

"Olivia," Elena said, her voice tense, "is the daughter of that Maria, your idiot uncle Andrei's whore; the woman who stole all our money! *That* Olivia!" Her fingers itched to break something as she breathed those words.

"Well open it then," Alina urged, leaning over the counter. "What does it say?"

Elena had to calm herself for a moment. She knew that her daughter was not the sharpest knife in the toolbox. With quick but steady breaths, Elena straightened out the letter, her eyes hooded as they moved from side to side. Her lips moved as she read, as if mouthing a silent prayer, then her eyes widened with shock.

"What?" Alina said. "What does it say?"

Elena ignored her as her legs shook so hard she almost fell over. She reached for the counter to support herself, knocking over a few utensils in the process, the noise clanking in the small space.

"It-it's from Olivia," Elena muttered slowly.

Alina shook her head quickly, her lips glistening with her red lipstick. "I know that already, Mom. But what does it say?"

Straightening, her face as plain as she could make it, Elena explained: "She says she's sorry for the loss of my brother, and she would like to come visit to discuss urgent business regarding Andrei's . . ." Her breathing faltered, her words quaked, and her right hand tightened into a fist. "Andrei's inheritance."

Alina jumped and squealed, her mouth wide open. She pumped her hands in the air.

"Does this mean we're rich now?" she wondered excitedly, moving quickly around the room.

Elena stood by the counter, the letter squeezed in her left hand. She bit her lips and shook her head, grinding her teeth against each other.

"Stop your nonsense!" Elena said.

Alina halted, gazing up in confusion.

Elena balled the letter in her hand, pressing it tight against the skin of her palm. "We don't want her American charity. We want every penny of what's owed to us!"

CHAPTER FOUR

T he rain pattered hard on the roof and the dark night lit up with the occasional flashes of lightning. It was so cold that Christian stretched an old, torn woolen blanket over his body. Then it hit him: the leaks!

With a moan, he rolled out of bed and picked up three metal buckets from a shelf in the dark hallway and carefully navigated the small farmhouse he shared with his mother and younger sisters. He knew the notorious spots in the little house and didn't even have to carry a lamp before he heard the low *drip-drop* sound.

"There you are: culprit number one." He looked up at the ceiling where a dark spot formed and the rained dripped through. A drop caught his face as he placed a small bucket under the leak.

There was another spot in the living room, and this one was worse than the first. The drops fell much faster, tapping the stone floor like a drum. They'd already created a small pool of water, which threatened to start flowing as soon as a few more drops settled in. The metal bucket clanked when Christian placed it down. He grabbed a mop.

"You're quite the stubborn one, aren't you, culprit number two?" he muttered, sliding the mop over the patch of water until the floor glistened. The *tap-tap* sound became a deep *clank* when he shifted the bucket under the trail of water.

"You'll be full by morning at this rate," he said and skipped over to the last spot by the door in the small kitchen.

On his way back to bed, he dropped by the small room his sisters shared. Standing by the doorway, he smiled fondly when he saw the four little bodies spread out on the two mattresses they shared. For a moment, he watched them stir quietly even while it rained and thundered outside. He'd do anything to keep the storm at bay, to let them sleep in peace.

His eyes went to the worn curtains, which were snapping from the blowing cold night air. He left the room and came back a moment later with two extra blankets—one of them his own. Quietly, he stepped into the room, past the shadows of stuffed animals and old dolls, and spread the blankets over them, tucking all four of them in. He stepped back and took one last look at them, then he too went off to sleep.

***

The next morning, Christian opened his eyes as the rising sun spilled through the cracked glass of his window. He pushed off the sweaters he'd used as a makeshift blanket and scanned his more-than-modest room—with not much more than a wooden desk and bed—for new leaks. Nothing. He sighed in relief.

"Time to start the new day," he said with a yawn and got out of bed. Peeking out the window, he saw the glisten of wet grass shining in the sun. The day was clear, warm, and pleasant.

Christian stretched out his long arms and felt his muscles loosen. He bent over and touched his toes and turned to his left and his right, the cracks along his spine like little knocks on wood. He rubbed his hand over his bare chest, subconsciously sliding his finger across the small scar close to his neck—an accident he'd had with a nail when he was young. His daily manual labor gave him his athletic build, his arms strong and bulging, his height at six feet even.

"That's a good thing, you know?" his mother would always tell him when he was younger. "Women like tall, strong men." His chin had the beginnings of a black stubble, which he would shave off soon. His hair was trimmed, dark, and smooth. Not long enough to make a man bun like the warriors in those fancy American movies, but nice and practical and neat.

While rubbing his back, Christian turned to his worn-out mattress and cast an accusing glance at it. "This one's your fault."

He picked up a white shirt and slipped his arms through it, linking together the four buttons that were left on it and heading for the door, but not before taking a glance in the mirror at himself. "Looking like a man who will land a big tour today," he said. Then he walked out the door, having to bend slightly under the low-hanging doorframe.

The buckets in the living room had filled with water from the rain last night, with the larger bucket almost spilling over. He grabbed them and went outside, dumping out the contents. Even though he knew the roof needed fixing—again—he didn't let that dampen his spirits as he reached for the last bucket and tossed the water.

The air smelled of freshly cut grass. Their old, white farmhouse was located in a small village in Transylvania. It wasn't much, the old house, but it was home and home always gave him a sense of security. Once in a while, when he had some free time, he'd carry planks and nails, clutching a hammer between his teeth, and try to fix the "bad spots" in the old house. Technically, almost every part was a "bad spot," but since his father had suddenly passed of a heart attack a few years back, the duty of keeping up the place and taking care of his mother and four sisters fell entirely on him—which he accepted wholeheartedly.

Christian stared up at the sky. The sun cast warm rays over the grass and the aged, mossy wooden barns. Birds fluttered past, chirping and circling in the air. They reminded him of his days as a little boy, when he'd played in haystacks and chased butterflies with other village children through the market crowds and the idyllic, small alleyways.

He walked toward the barn's red, wooden gates, behind which he could hear the deep snorting of their cow.

"Good morning, old lady," he greeted the cow as he pushed open the squeaky barn doors. "May I request some of your milk?" He patted the large, friendly animal's face. The cow grunted and mooed at him.

"I'll take that as a yes," he said and took a seat on a shaky wooden stool and settled the bucket under the cow. "Don't know what we'd do without you." He squirted fresh milk into the bucket. They'd had to sell most of their livestock when his father passed away. Moomoo, as the girls called her, and a few chickens were all that they had left.

"Thanks for the milk," he said and patted the cow, again receiving a low grunt. His sisters had often chided him for talking to the animals like a crazy person.

"They sense your feelings," he'd told them. "So if you're sad or angry or unhappy, they know."

"Really?" the girls had asked, wide-eyed.

He'd nodded. It was what his dad had told him when he was a boy, and he'd accepted it as truth.

He moved along the barn to the chicken coop, the steady clucking of the birds ringing through the air. The hens were all pecking around, some sitting on stacks of hay.

"Morning, ladies." Christian scanned the coop. He grinned when he spotted the eggs, but his smile wavered when he counted just six of them. Not enough for everybody, again. He placed the eggs carefully into his basket.

"I'm sure we can do much better tomorrow, ladies," Christian said to the chickens as he carried the eggs and the bucket of fresh milk to the house.

He was in the kitchen, a cramped room with old flower wallpaper and outdated appliances, making breakfast when he first heard the thumping of feet and the tiny voices of the girls. The eggs sizzled in the pan while he whistled and moved from one corner of the tiny kitchen to the other, picking up the tin of salt and pepper.

Not long after, he balanced four plates into the corner space with a wooden table and chairs which served for a dining area.

"Breakfast's ready, ladies," he called out, and his sisters scrambled in, each pushing back a chair and getting seated. He smiled at them as he set the plates in front of their beaming faces and golden forelocks. To him, they looked like angels, as if any moment they would spread sparkling white wings and fly off.

"Hope yougher've made your beds? You know the law," he said with a warm smile.

The girls nodded in an almost-perfect synchronized manner. Christian watched them dig into their breakfast of eggs and sausages, then he turned to see his mother wheeling in. He glanced at the wheel-chair, something she only used on days she felt too weak to walk. *She is having a bad day again,* he thought. She was such a beauty once and always full of energy. Her hair had been golden as the sun, her face elegant and fine. What he saw in front of him now could not be further from that bright memory. Her hair looked oily and unwashed, the pink lipstick on her lips uneven from her shaking hands. But she hated it when he made a big deal about her health, so he pretended everything was fine, looking almost as sharp as before.

"You're looking bright this morning," he said, trying to sound cheerful. She smiled faintly and looked at him. She'd developed multiple sclerosis not long after his father had passed away. They almost lost her too. It had been a dark time that still haunted him at night sometimes.

Her bright blue eyes still gazing at him, his mother moved her lips slowly. "Have you had anything for breakfast yet?" she asked, her words coming out slowly, breathlessly. He smiled and held her hand.

"Of course I have, right before the girls woke up," he lied. "Your majesty," he added, and straightened his spine when he heard his sisters laugh, mumbling to each other with mouths full.

"Ah-ah, what did I say about talking with full mouths? What are you going to do if a prince invited you to dine at this golden table? Spit all over his crystal dishes?"

His sisters giggled some more, then focused on their breakfast.

Christian watched his mother eat for a few minutes before excusing himself.

"Are you sure you don't need more food?" his mother hollered after him in a shaky voice as he made his way down the dark corridor of cracked walls littered with sun-bleached family portraits.

"I'm stuffed, mother," he answered and stepped into his room to grab his suit jacket, the nice dark blue one. His stomach was growling, but what was the use of making them feel guilty? He would grab a piece of dry bread and an apple on his way to work, content that he had food at all.

Being the man of the house meant a lot of things, and making sure that the little they had wouldn't vanish was one of them. His job paid for the electric and the medical bills, for the heat and the girls' school materials.

Christian prided himself in his job. He worked as a private tour guide, using the English it had taken him years to learn. The competition had been fierce, but he'd managed to get the job with his charm and language skills—and he loved it. Listening to the tourists and their tales from faraway places was the most exciting thing in the world to him. *Someday I will see them all with my own eyes,* he'd tell himself, almost believing it at times.

He stood outside the house as the sun reflected off the chipped white paint of his rusty, old minibus. He ran his hand over the dented body, carefully peeling off dirt and strands of grass from his last bumpy tour. The words 'DISCOVERY ROMANIA' were painted on the bus, the Y crossed out with red paint. He'd tried painting over it, but it always seemed to surface again, making it look even worse. He'd gotten the bus from a neighbor who'd used to it sell chickens. And his neighbor had gotten it from someone else. He wasn't sure how many hands the bus had been through, but he was sure it had been well loved.

"Today is a good day," he said and patted the side of the bus, moving over to the driver's side. The door creaked open; at this point, he didn't have to use a key to open it, just a simple tap would do the trick.

Business had been slow for a while now; actually, it had never picked up in the first place, to be honest. This had nothing to do with his charisma or English skills, or charming looks, as his mom insisted. Looking at his bus, Christian knew what the culprit was.

"Christian, your bus smokes and is as rusty as Alexandru's crazy old widow," his rivals in the tourist business always mocked him.

Holding the creaking door, ready to heave himself in, Christian knew that they were right. This bus needed to go if he wanted business to get better—but business had to get better for the bus to go.

"Off to work," he said to himself and was about to close the door when he heard Sofia, the youngest of his little sisters.

"Don't go," she said.

He turned around to see her skipping toward him. She leaped onto the door and clung to the open window.

"Stay and play." She looked up at him with a grin, showing her missing front tooth. She had just turned four and acted not a day older.

He chuckled and picked her up to heave her into the bus and onto his lap. "I have to go to work, sweetie, but I'll be back soon."

He spotted another of his sisters, Daria, running up to him and sighed. "You ladies are like ants, huh? Where there's one . . ."

"Is it true that vampires live in Dracula's castle?" Sofia asked as she helped Daria, who was one year older, climb into the van and squeeze herself onto the seat next to Christian.

"You're going to see Dracula again without us?" Daria shouted, almost mad. Suddenly he saw the other two storm out, Ana and Gabriele. His sisters were about a year apart, ranging from four to eight-years-old, with Sofia being the youngest and Ana the oldest.

"He's going to Dracula's ghost with the rich foreigners again?" Ana's high-pitched voice piped accusingly. She waited for Gabriele to open the back passenger door of the van for her. Christian sighed and looked behind him to see Ana and Gabriele already sitting in the back.

"Why do you never take us with you? We want to meet Dracula too." Gabriele crossed her arms.

Christian made a serious face and spoke in a low voice. "Have you forgotten? I have to feed him the rich tourists before you can meet him. Otherwise, he'll eat you too." The older girls, Sofia and Daria, giggled, but Gabriele and Ana's eyes widened.

"Why doesn't he eat you then?" Sofia asked, hands on her hips.

"You want to know, huh? Well then," he said with a smile, turning around for a few seconds. "Because he only drinks the blood of beautiful princesses like you!" He hissed, baring his teeth like a vampire. The girls screamed in delight and jumped out of the van, scattering out on the front yard. Christian got out too and chased after them until he'd tickled each, hissing like a vampire as he did. The girls squealed and laughed.

"Girls!" Their mom appeared at the front door. "Stop bothering your brother!"

Christian straightened his back, held his waist, and pretended to be out of breath.

"All right, we'll have to finish this some other time, beauties," he said. The girls each came running to give him a hug. This was one of the moments that made the whole struggle worth it, seeing the smiles on their faces and hearing the joy in their voices. His eyes went to his mother, who was watching the scene with a sad smile.

"Girls, please go and clean your dishes," she said. The girls all sighed, but one by one ran inside to do as they were told. His mother waited a moment longer, watching as the girls disappeared into the kitchen, then she turned back to Christian.

"You can't keep staying here," she suddenly said.

He looked away. "Not this again, Mom."

"It's not fair for you," she continued calmly, pausing to catch her breath. "You should move to the big city, go to university, and live your life."

"I'm living my life, Mom," he responded and walked over to her. "You and the girls are my life."

"You should study and find yourself a wife, have children, Christian," she said.

He reached to take her hand, but she moved it away, setting it on the scarf around her neck.

"I could never just leave you. Father would want it this way, I know it."

Her face grew soft again. "Your father would agree with me, that's what I know." She took a deep breath. Christian cast a concerned gaze at her. She looked at him and sighed. He saw that sad look in her eyes and smiled.

"Enough of this talk," he said. "Today is a good day, I can feel it. I'm sure there are lines of rich tourists waiting for me as we speak."

His mother raised a brow at him, but Christian grinned even wider and cleared his throat to imitate a woman's voice: "Where is that handsome young Romanian tour guide, Christian? The one who got his good looks from his mother. I want to give him all my money to take me to Dracula's castle."

His mother laughed.

"Business is picking up," he lied. "I mean, I'm taking a British family out on a tour today and they're going to pay good euros for it. That's something, right? And I love the job."

The hopeful look in his mother's eyes brightened.

"I just need a few more of these," he continued, rubbing the back of his head to distract himself from the lies. His mother grinned brightly, the smile lines on her face drawing together.

"I better go now. I don't want Luca, that slimy snail, stealing my tourists again. I love you."

She reached out and patted his hand. Her palm was rough and cold as she smiled at him. "Yes, go, that Luca is as slimly as they get. God will be with you," she said, her voice steadier and much more relaxed. He leaned in and kissed her forehead.

"I'll be back for lunch. Or maybe dinner," he said.

On his way to the van, he heard his sisters' playful voices coming from the inside of the house, so he rushed into the driver's seat and closed the door. Once inside, he looked at himself in the rearview mirror and sighed deeply, a frown on his face.

That British family would have been nice to have, he thought to himself, but he knew that it would be a regular day of fighting over the tourists with the other guides—and their vans were new and shiny and had working AC.

Christian started the van and drove off before his sisters could jump him once more. The bus bounced down the road past lush green hills and dense forest. It was a beautiful day. His destination was a small historic town that would bring all the tourists from Bucharest on the train. It was about an hour from his own small village. He smiled as he drove in, taking in the sights of the town. Its colorful medieval buildings lined the cobbled stone roads. Little businesses popped up around the various corners, tables surrounding bright umbrellas and carts full of shiny trinkets and fancy souvenirs for tourists. Flapping flags of blue and yellow hung over the streets. Christian smiled and remembered when his father used to take him to town when he was younger. He would stare at those flags and enjoy the laughter and haggling around him, and the smell of fresh food and fruits.

Things had changed since then. The cities and larger towns were where young people went now, replacing the crowds of the Romanian countryside with tourists. He thought about his mother's words while he drove.

"I can't leave," he said aloud, the gearshift creaking as he pressed down on the clutch and switched gears, flooring the gas pedal, which grumbled noisily without a significant increase in speed.

"They need me," he muttered as if trying to convince himself. "I can't leave."

**

It was a sunny, late summer day. The plaza in the middle of town was buzzing: tourists marching out of the train station and large buses with bold words and pictures splashed on them. Tour guides and souvenir shop owners were scrambling for those tourists, reaching out and sputtering well-rehearsed phrases, some with notoriously bad English.

Gothic churches and medieval stone buildings dominated the downtown plaza, but none piqued the interest of the tourists as much as the famed Bran Castle, spooky home of Vlad the Impaler, a.k.a. Dracula. The funny thing was, according to most historians, Dracula had actually never stepped foot in this castle. But, like most other tour guides, Christian kept telling tourists about all the horrors that took place in the dungeons and that, because of the lack of written accounts from that era, no one could prove that Dracula *didn't* commit them with his own murderous hands. That was good enough for most tourists to dish out the hundred euros for the four-hour roundtrip on the minibuses.

Christian scanned around for a spot to park, exhaling slowly and trying to ignore the looks and comments his van always got when he drove into town. It was the one good thing about his engine being so loud—he couldn't hear what they were saying. He slammed his hand against the center of the wheel, forcing the croaking horn to let out a blast. It scattered the gawkers, who waved their fists at him, their mouths moving like a TV show on mute.

The problem was the horn didn't stop once he lifted his hand from the wheel. *I need to stop honking like this,* he told himself as the loud blare tore through the air, attracting all eyes to him. He smacked the steering wheel, hoping it would quiet. It didn't. He frowned at how he must look to potential customers: a rickety, smoky bus bouncing down the road, honking ceaselessly.

Christian sighed and reached down the side of the wheel till his fingers grazed the group of exposed wires, most of which used to have a function but had now been snipped off. He connected the horn to the battery and the honking died.

The other fancy tour vans were parked in a line, which made it almost an act of war once the tourists came along. It was every tour guide for himself. Some of the more aggressive guides would approach the tourists and grab them by their arms, sweet-talking them until they were safely seated in their vans. Christian never did that; he thought it was harassment.

Christian parked his old bus along the row of colorful, semi-new, and downright fancy minivans. His creaked and spurted out thick smoke and backfired before coming to a halt. The other drivers, old bald Luca leading them, laughed at the sight of Christian.

"It's smokin' Chrisi," Luca hollered, his round belly moving up and down with each laugh. He had a white towel draped around his sweaty neck, which he occasionally dabbed his face with. "Here to snatch all the tourists again?"

"It's as ancient as this town," another skinny guide in a polo shirt chimed in, glancing at Christian's van. They all laughed.

Christian smiled and folded his arms. "Well, that means it fits right in, just like me, here to stay . . . forever." Christian grinned. The other drivers stopped laughing. He knew what they really were doing. If they could get him to quit, it would be one less tour guide to battle with. Most of these jokers understood that if he had a better bus, they wouldn't be able to compete with him: He was good with people, he knew his history, and his English was solid.

The train finally arrived and the guides, including Christian, became alert, like lions ready to pounce on unwitting prey. They started moving closer to the train station and the street that led to the plaza. After a few moments, a fresh swarm of tourists flooded out of the train. It was a diverse swarm, this round, filled with families, older couples with cameras hanging around their necks, and the golden ticket of the tour bus business: large Asian groups. Their faces were full of awe, their cameras constantly snapping, just begging to take in these sights that were oh-so-different from their own cities. But Christian's bus was too small for them anyway, so he let the others jumped on them as he approached a middle-aged couple holding a travel guide with large red letters on it—*Europe*. The man had a suspicious look on his face as soon as he spotted Christian. His eyes went to his wife and the look intensified.

"How about a tour of my beautiful city? Dracula's castle is not far from here," Christian said with a smile, his English smooth and error-free. The woman blinked her long eyelashes and smiled at her husband, but the man grunted, regarding him closely.

"How much?" he asked in an American accent as he scratched his brown beard.

Christian opened his mouth, but before he could speak, Luca shouted out in broken English: "Hey Christian, are you sure your AC is fixed? It'll get hot today." He nodded up to the bright, cloudless blue sky. "Very hot," he added, his bald head glittering like a polished bowling ball as he overdramatically wiped his white towel over his face.

"You don't have AC?" the American man frowned and glared at Christian's bus.

"No, but we won't be staying in the bus all day, sir. And with the windows down—"

"How about I take your friends on a tour for you?" Luca chipped in innocently.

"Thank you, Luca, but I've got this," Christian said.

The American tourist frowned. "Sorry my friend, but I need AC."

Luca rushed over to his bus and opened the door. "My bus is temperature controlled and even has USB charger ports for you. Come along, I will split this fare with my good friend Christian for referring you." Luca smirked at Christian, who could do nothing but watch helplessly as the couple followed Luca. Luca wouldn't split anything with him, that was a bunch of bull.

Another client gone. Christian ran his hand through his hair.

He kept trying, each time using his charm and witticism on the prospective clients, but all that wouldn't matter as soon as they saw his bus.

"Get yourself a better van, pal, and I'd love that tour of yours," one tourist said with a friendly smile and gave him ten euros. Christian imagined how much the man would have paid if he'd been the one to take him to Bran castle. He knew his tours were better than Luca's. He had studied at home for years to perfect his English and learn all the history of the region, but with a bus like this . . .

"Just one tour is all I need," Christian kept telling himself while he waited, the sun hotter now and the town bustling with people. He felt a slight pang in his stomach—hunger—but ignored it. Now's not the time, he told himself. Then he saw the group of women—or heard them. They were loud, laughing a lot, and speaking quickly. As expected, he was not the only one to notice the opportunity. Three other tour guides already swarmed around them like bees over a soda, but for some reason the five women brushed them away and headed straight for Christian. At first glance, they looked as if they were college students from abroad. They were colorfully dressed in short pants, tank tops, dresses, and lots of makeup, and they wouldn't stop giggling. One of them, a tall blonde, had a bottle of vodka in one hand with her purse clutched in the other. Christian smiled; he liked seeing people out and enjoying their lives.

"Hey, pretty boy," the tall blonde one said and came to a stop awkwardly close to him, her blue eyes sparkling as she checked him out. She turned around, her tight dress clasping her rounded frame, and shouted to the others: "What a village beauty!"

The other girls laughed and surrounded him with loud giggles and flushed faces.

"He's such a cutie. Can we keep you?" another joked, taking a sip from a red plastic cup.

"A sexy cutie," Christian heard from behind him and jolted when he felt a hand slip over his stomach. He stepped back so that the ladies were all in front of him. He gave them his charming smile and spoke politely.

"Hello ladies, how about a tour of Dracula's castle? Its dungeon is—"

"Have a drink with us first," the tall blonde one blurted out. The others hooted and laughed and held their cups up to his face, urging him to do just that. His smile remained plastered on his face. He'd seen this sort of thing before, tourists having a little too much fun. No harm done. He was sure he could handle it, and he needed the money.

Rubbing his hands together, he took a tiny step forward and went through his catch lines, but the ladies weren't even listening; they were refilling their cups instead.

"Don't be so boring, cutie, drink with us!" Christian turned to see a brown-haired girl with an oval face and pink lipstick.

The others laughed, and the blonde one tumbled forward: "Show us your six pack," she mumbled, her speech slurred. Her fellow party warrior girlfriend, the brown-haired one, placed a hand on his chest. He caught the sharp scent of her perfume mixed with the stench of alcohol.

"How about this: we'll go on your tour if you party with us after." The others grinned and shifted closer, mumbling words of agreement.

"What do you say, pretty village boy?"

Christian looked past the girls at the other tour guides watching them closely, knowing they'd pounce as soon as he let these women go. He sighed and bit his lip. While he stared at them, they giggled continuously, puckering their lips, and one even ran a finger over his face. He sighed again. *There's no way I'm taking these women on a tour,* he thought.

"So . . . what's it gonna be, sexy boy?" the blonde one asked as she tilted her head back and took a long swig, the clear liquid spilling down her cheeks.

Christian slowly backed away, shaking his head in regret.

"I'm sorry but my, uh . . ." His eyes went to his bus. "I don't drink and drive." Which was the truth. If anything happened to these women, he would feel responsible. Besides, he wasn't into getting sexually harassed for hours. Some men might make use of a situation like this, exploit these pretty young women, but he wasn't one of them. His father had raised him to never treat a woman any different than he'd want his mother and sisters to be treated.

He felt a tug on his arm and a sharp pinch of fingernails. "Then we just drink."

"Maybe some other time, ladies," he assured them. "Would you like me to drop you off back at your hotel? I won't charge you for that. It might be better to have your fun there."

The ladies frowned in disappointment.

"What are you, my mother?" the blonde one barked and started toward the eagerly welcoming hands of another tour guide. But instead of stopping, she passed them and stumbled into a small grocery store—probably to get more alcohol.

"You're boring," the one with the pink lipstick said and gave his butt a tap, then stumbled off with the others.

He exhaled as they all went into the store. A few minutes later, the ladies came back out with more booze in their hands. Some of them waved at him on their way to the plaza.

"Bye cutie," one of them hollered.

"It was the right thing to do," he muttered after they'd disappeared into the plaza crowd. A bit deflated, Christian walked back to his bus to eat some of the dry bread and the apple he had packed for lunch. He bit into the rock-hard white bread. It had never tasted so stale.

***

Elena Rusu pinched her lips from where she stood outside a local bakery, watching the group of girls practically molest Christian, one of the tour boys. Even some locals stopped to look and mutter excitedly with one another. Her lips twitched as she longed to join in with her own remarks.

"I can see why they're all over him," one older woman said in the local dialect as she placed her grocery bags on the ground with a loud grunt. "He is pretty, Antonia's boy."

"His father was too, back in the day," another added and went about her businesses. Elena had kept her eyes on Christian as the foreign women fussed over him like dogs in heat.

"It's because they have money. Money excuses everything," Elena said to the woman who was now bending over again to pick up her groceries.

"Money, money, money . . . that's all that counts in this world today. Aside from a pretty boy like Christian, only that might count even more," the old woman mumbled and left, her grocery bags dangling around her wrists.

An idea was forming in Elena's head. She wasn't sure what it was yet, so she played with it, all while staring at Christian.

With slow steps, Elena approached him. Christian was leaning against his bus, eating a piece of bread with those perfect lips of his.

She smiled at him when she got close. He leaned off the bus when he saw her and smiled back.

"Elena, don't tell me you need a tour."

"No."

He nodded, still smiling, looking incredibly handsome.

"Well not for me, at least."

His smile faded as he cocked his head. "Who then? Alina?"

Elena shook her head. "I'll tell you on the way to my house. I'll pay for the ride."

Christian frowned. "Are you ill? I can drop you off at home, no need to pay."

Elena's eyes went to his rusty bus. "Doesn't look like you can afford to drive people around for free," she added unable to keep the mocking tone from her voice. "Do you want the money or not?"

He pinched his lips, then nodded.

"How is your mother? How is Antonia?" Elena asked after sitting down in the front seat and slamming the creaking door shut.

Christian rubbed his head before touching the wires beneath the steering wheel. The bus jolted alive with sharp screeches and coughs.

"She's okay. Has good days and bad days," he said. Then he took one quick look at her and put the vehicle in gear. "I'm sorry for your loss, by the way. I heard your brother passed."

"He was an idiot, but thank you," she said, pulling a cigarette and lighter from her purse. She was about to light it, but Christian shook his head.

"Are you kidding me?" she barked as the bus spewed smoke through the cracked windows.

"Alright. Fair enough," he mumbled.

Elena studied him, his thick hair and symmetrical face. He was as sweet as he was handsome, all of the town knew it. If only he had a vehicle to match. "I don't know how you make any money with this pile of junk," she said.

When they got to her small home, Christian ran around the bus to open the door for her.

"I have a distant relative coming to visit from America," she said as she accepted his help out of the bus.

"I didn't know you had family in America besides Andrei."

"Well, I said distant, didn't I? Anyway, I'd love for you to take her on a tour around Transylvania while she's here. I'll pay you well for it."

He frowned. Elena Rusu was one of the poorest souls in town. He looked over her shoulder at the crumbling house behind her. Then his eyes snapped back to her. "Sure. I can do that. No need to pay if it's just a day or two."

Elena felt heat rush into her cheeks. Even a poor church mouse like Christian pitied her. "Keep your charity for the other fools in this village. I'm prepared to give you five thousand euros for it," she said, lifting her chin.

"Are you joking? Five thousand euros?" He frowned at her, taking a quick peek at the rundown little house. He opened his mouth but closed it again.

Elena looked down her nose at him. "My brother, you idiot. I inherited a lot of money."

He blinked quickly then nodded. Of course. Everybody knew Andrei Rusu around here.

"But if you're not interested, I can very well hire someone else. Luca maybe?" She moved away from the bus and started walking toward her house when she heard his hasty footsteps behind her. She grinned before he reached her.

"I'm sorry," he said.

She straightened her face before turning around. "You should be. Look at your van! I'm only considering you because I know your mother. You could show some gratitude."

He apologized again, rubbing his hands together. "I honestly didn't mean it that way, Elena. I'm grateful for the opportunity, I really am."

"Good. Get back here this evening and we'll talk about details," Elena said and opened the door to her house without looking at him, closing it behind her in the same fashion. Then she rushed over to her living room window and watched through the stained white curtains as Christian jumped into his bus. She watched the creaking bus whine several times and shook her head in disbelief when Christian jumped down and had to give the bus a little push before jumping right back in. The stupid thing suddenly blasted a long honk, which didn't stop until the bus was out of sight, turning around the corner of a farm-house.

"Perfect," Elena said, a smile turning the corners of her cracked lips.

CHAPTER FIVE

O livia watched the plane dip through the blue sky as they arrived at the Bucharest airport. She was relieved to be able to stretch her legs. The flight was long, and although Mr. Stanley had booked her in business class, she'd been unable to get any sleep. Her emotions were running high the moment she got on the plane in Boston. The mixture of excitement and anxiousness she felt about coming to her mother's home country was too overwhelming to even think of sleep.

She yawned as she got off the plane. The airport looked like any other, with high ceilings, glass windows, and elevators running up and down between floors. People pushed trolleys, talked into phones, and rushed by in order to make their flight. Olivia got into one of the glass elevators that led to baggage claim, watching every sign closely, searching for instructions in English. Grumbling at how slow the elevator was, Olivia leaned against its glass wall and looked down below at the baggage claim area. Suddenly she spotted her bright yellow bag—in the hands of a woman with red hair. Wasn't that the same woman who was engaging her in chit-chat in front of the lavatory on the plane?

"Wait, what?" She blinked. She wasn't mistaken; she could spot her bright yellow bag anywhere. It had been a Christmas gift from her mother, and now it was in the hands of a stranger. She watched as the woman with red hair walked away from baggage claim, Olivia's bag in hand.

"Hey! That's my bag!" She banged against he the glass before realizing how pointless it was yelling through the elevator walls. "Move faster already!" she demanded, repeatedly pressing her hands on the down button. The elevator finally stopped, but by then, the woman had already disappeared.

Olivia did a little dance in front of the slowly opening elevator doors and squeezed through the crack the moment the doors were wide enough to fit through. She bolted past baggage claim, bumping into a person or two, and headed for customs. She caught the eyes of a tall, bulky customs agent, who was watching her with a surprised look on his face.

"Help!" Olivia shouted. "Someone stole my bag!"

***

Christian noted the odd looks people gave him when they saw his ancient van parked by the cabs at the airport. He ignored it with a smile, and nearly asked them if they needed a ride. He flipped the sign in his hand and stared at it for a moment, at the words printed on it: OLIVIA CARTER.

He wondered what the American lady would look like and how Elena was actually related to her. But then, everybody was a distant relative in Romania. It was custom to talk acquaintances up, even the ones you'd never met or had no real blood connection with.

"She said she's going to be carrying a bright yellow bag," Elena had told him, so he looked out for the bag.

The automatic glass doors to the airport opened again and a woman with red hair and a bright yellow bag stormed out. Christian straightened up and watched her.

Bright yellow bag. That had to be her. Why was she in such a hurry? He waved her over when he saw her moving in his direction. Holding the sign, he smiled at her.

"Are you Olivia? I'm here to pick you up."

The woman peeked over her shoulder then back at the sign. She nodded, smiling, and hastily got into the van with her luggage in hand. Maybe it wasn't custom to put bags into the trunk in America. He shrugged and closed the door behind her. But just as he stepped into the driver's seat and started the smoky engine, he heard a woman's voice yell outside the airport. Only moments later, a very similar-looking woman banged on the side of his van. She looked angry and was breathing hard. She had brown hair and panicked eyes. If not strikingly attractive, she was cute with her red huffing cheeks. She was maybe a few years older than he was. Her black coat had fallen off one of her shoulders, exposing a white wool sweater. Her fiery eyes met Christian's.

"What the . . ." Christian muttered. He had his hand on the steering wheel when the woman rushed to his side, brows drawn tightly, face flushed. He quickly locked the doors to his van, just in time as the woman grabbed his driver side's handle and pulled on it without success.

"Where do you think you're going with my bag, you thieves!"

"Wait, what?" Christian blurted.

"My bag, you're stealing my bag!" the woman yelled. Shaking his head, he gently tapped his foot on the gas paddle to rev the engine. The van slowly started rolling.

"Step aside, please," he asked her. "No tours today," he added, thinking maybe it was a crazy drink tourist. But the woman let out a sarcastic laugh.

"Unbelievable!" she shouted and jumped in front of his van, blocking the way.

"Get out of the way," Christian shouted as he stepped hard on the brakes and the van screeched to a sudden stop.

"That woman right there," the hysterical woman shouted, pointing at the red-haired woman. "She stole my bag!"

Confused, Christian stared into the crazy woman's eyes, held captive for a moment by the green-brown color of them. Then he turned to the woman in the back of the van. The red-haired Olivia Carter shrugged at him with a frown.

"Sorry to ask you this," Christian said, scratching his neck, "but do you have an ID on you?"

The woman nodded and pulled out a blue leather purse and fumbled through different items and cards in it. Then she smiled and held up an American driver's license. Her thumb was half-covering the picture, but the name clearly stated Olivia Carter.

Christian faced the hysterical woman again.

"You . . . you stole my wallet too!" the crazy woman yelled. Christian let out an exasperated sigh. He let down the window a crack, just enough for the woman outside to hear him.

"I have a job to do, lady. Please move away from my van." He was trying his best to remain calm, but the woman quickly fired angry words at him:

"Fine job you have there, stealing from people! Where's the police!" the woman yelled and stepped, frantically looking around. This was his chance.

Taking a deep breath, Christian threw the woman a last, empathetic glance and hit the gas pedal. A few moments later, the loud van screeched away. For some reason, Christian kept his eyes on the cracked side rear mirror, watching the woman flap her hands in protest, her lips moving fast, but her words were drowned out by his backfiring engine. For some reason, Christian felt bad for her.

Then he redirected his gaze to the rearview mirror. Looking at Olivia, he chuckled with a slow shake of his head. "That was crazy, huh? I'm sorry for that. There are some smart thieves here, but don't think that's how we all are in Romania. Most people are good, honest, and hard-working." His eyes went to the road and back to Olivia after he got no response from her. Hopefully, she wasn't too shaken by the whole incident, he thought. American women were among the strongest on this planet from what he had read and seen in the movies. Something like this wouldn't traumatize her, would it? Besides, she looked calm enough, eyes fixed ahead and lips pressed tight into a smile. Yet, something about that silence unsettled him.

"By the way, how was the flight? Is the food on board as bad as the tourists say?"

Olivia briefly looked at him and averted her gaze instantly, peering at the windshield as if the various branching cracks had something interesting to say. She smiled and nodded without looking at him.

His eyes narrowed. That was such a simple question and the Americans he'd come in contact with would never hesitate to muse about their flights' shitty food or cheap booze.

Christian grinned into the mirror. "You don't understand a word I'm saying, do you?"

Olivia smiled and nodded again. Christian felt his heart skip a beat and gripped the steering wheel tightly.

"Goddamn it!"

He jerked the wheel to maneuver his bus onto the safety lane and slammed his foot on the brakes. A cab behind swerved and emerged from the thick cloud of smoke, the driver laying on his horn and swearing out his window. Christian shouted back apologies and brought the bus to a complete halt.

The woman's hands slowly fumbling with the purse while her right hand crept for the handle of the backdoor. He noticed the movement and was about to reach for her when she pushed the door open and jumped out. Reacting quickly, Christian stretched his hand and grabbed the woman's purse, which was entangled with her arm. Her red hair bounced, and she turned and glared at him, eyes flashing. She pulled and tore at the straps of the purse, but Christian held on firmly.

"Look," he said in Romanian, breathing hard and already tired of this day. "Just get out of here and leave what's not yours."

The woman hesitated, glared at him like a wild animal. Christian sighed.

"You know I'm faster than you are. Do you really want me to chase you and hold you here until the police arrives?"

She seemed to mellow at the mention of the *police*.

"Asshole!" she growled in Romanian and let go of the purse. It snapped back into the bus. She flipped him off, the red nail polish glaring, and ran off. He watched her running down the side of the road then reached for the blue purse and opened it. His brown eyes stared at the photo on the American driver's license. It was definitely the crazy lady. His head and his heart thumped.

"This is bad, bad, bad . . . you idiot!" He'd made a humungous mistake.

"Olivia Carter," he muttered, looking at the name on the license, the letters staring back at him accusingly.

"I can't believe this." He shifted the gears, turning the bus around. The wheels squeaked and screeched and churned up thick smoke as he tore back down the road, heading straight for the airport—the last place on Earth he wanted to be.

CHAPTER SIX

Olivia didn't think that her day could get any worse. First her luggage and wallet had been stolen, now she found herself in a stuffy office at the airport, trying to convince the police officers that she wasn't crazy. She'd gone over her explanation several times and now they were going to make her do it again.

"I've told you," she said in a voice cracked from shouting, "I'm not crazy."

"Yes, yes you've said that already," the police officer said as he looked at her like she was a psycho.

"But explain to me again, if this woman stole all your things, how come you still have your passport? It's the most valued item on the black market here."

He held it up like it was proof of something, which it wasn't!

She couldn't help her exasperated sigh as she clasped her hands together in her lap and bowed her head. Her necklace, a gift from her parents, slid out in the process and she thought of her mother. *I need strength, Mom,* she prayed and took a slow breath.

"As I've told you a million times, I put the passport in my jeans pocket after I filled out the European customs declaration card on board. We were about to land."

"Mm-hmm. Yes, you said that. And you didn't even notice that your purse was gone from your coat pocket?"

She sighed again and raised her head. "Yes. That is how it was. That red-haired lady must have stolen it when I was focusing on filling out that form. Or when I used the bathroom on the plane. I think she was also working with that other guy. The handsome driver."

The policemen exchanged quick glances. Olivia noticed and her throat clogged, coughing out the frustration. "Aren't you supposed to help me?" she added in a much-subdued voice.

The officer who held the passport, a tall young man with a black beard, was about to speak when the phone rang. He held up a finger in a "one moment" gesture and picked up.

"Hello?" he said in a flat, accented voice. He nodded and listened, then frowned and looked at Olivia. "Really?" he said in English and switched to Romanian for the final half-minute the call lasted.

"What?" Olivia asked. "Who was that?"

The door to the office opened, and two men walked in. She bit her lips and pinched the chair hard. One was another cop, and the other was the thief with the smoky bus.

"Yes, that's him! You found him!" she yelled. But nobody moved to make an arrest, and judging by the soft, embarrassed smile on the guy's handsome face, Olivia was pretty sure that no arrests were going to be made any time soon—or ever. Then why was the handsome thief even here? She felt the anger stirring fresh within her. Even more so now, she hated the way the word *handsome* kept popping into her head.

"One moment, Miss Carter," the police officer who'd just walked said before turning to his coworkers and speaking in Romanian. Olivia watched them with crossed arms. Occasionally her eyes would drift to the attractive thief, who was much taller than the police officer next to him—and their eyes would meet. He'd give her that embarrassed smile with those pretty lips and white teeth and she'd turn away.

Olivia recognized her blue purse when the other police officer brought it out and showed it to his coworker, muttering more words she couldn't understand. She did pick out "American," *or was it Americana or Americano?* She was clearly the one in the picture and she felt a refreshing wave of relief flood through her when the officers turned to her, this time with soft smiles on their faces.

"Really sorry for the inconvenience," one of them said in carefully constructed English. He sounded like a child, Olivia thought. She would have felt bad for thinking it, but these men deserved every condescending thought she had. She could have ended up in jail just because those jokers couldn't put one and one together. They wouldn't even let her call Mr. Stanley, rejecting the one thing she knew about getting arrested. Her one phone call!

Yet, this was not America, and mistakes happened, even ones as bad as this. So, she nodded and rose from her old plastic chair, grabbing her purse. She ignored the attractive man, who stood by the door as she walked past. Despite her fury, she was incredibly relieved that she wasn't about to end up in a Romanian prison cell.

"Miss Carter," the driver called after her. She kept walking.

"I'm not a thief. My name is Christian. I was uh . . . I was supposed to pick you up at the airport today before the, um, the little mix-up."

Olivia turned to face him. Because he was so tall, the first thing she saw was his chest, so she had to tilt her head up to meet his eyes.

"'Little mix-up'?" she repeated angrily. The man, Christian, ran his hand through his dark, thick hair, lost for words.

"*Big* mix-up?" he said.

Olivia raised a brow. "Where is my luggage?"

"Yes, of course. I have it. In my van. Let's go and get it, and then I can drive you—"

"I think I can take a cab from here. You've done enough, thanks."

She ignored the deflated look on his face.

"Your bag is this way." He started walking down the dark hallways of the airport's administrative offices. She followed as he slowed, adjusting his pace to hers.

"I'm so sorry about everything. If you think about it, I kinda did it for you, I mean, believing that woman was you, Olivia. I thought you were some crazy lady—"

"Crazy?" she stopped and scoffed, raising an eyebrow.

"I mean, not crazy as in *crazy*, but more like in a funny way. . ." he rambled, a look of desperation in his eyes. He sighed. "Please just listen to me for a second. I'm really sorry about all of this. It was a misunderstanding."

Olivia opened the small door at the end of the hallway that led to the *arrivals* section of the airport. The long line of yellow taxis and the tourists storming toward them distracted her for a second.

"Why don't we just start fresh?" Christian said. "I promise this will never happen again."

She looked at him briefly. His eyes were full of hope and desperation at the same time.

"Just let me drive you as I was supposed to, please. Elena will expect us back soon."

Olivia tightened her lips and her nose flared. The more she stared at him, the angrier she got. Yet, at the same time, the honest look on his face made her want to reconsider. She also didn't want to put Elena out if this was something she'd planned for her—Elena had been through enough after the loss of a loved one.

Olivia sighed. "Well . . . let's start with my luggage."

With a hopeful smile, he pointed at the van parked at the end of the line of taxis. "This way."

Olivia's mouth dropped slightly open at seeing the van. She'd been so focused on that red-haired lady and her stolen luggage, she hadn't fully taken in the monstrosity of the vehicle.

"It's not much," he said apologetically, "but it'll get us from A to B, I can promise you that."

Olivia glanced longingly at the cabs again. His gaze followed hers.

"Elena will be upset if I show up without you—worse if she finds out I let you go home in a taxi. Some of them will cheat you."

Gazing up at him and his pretty dark eyes, Olivia weighed her options once more. *Come on, it was a misunderstanding,* she told herself. *It's just a ride, not a marriage proposal.*

"Fine," she said in friendlier tone. "You can drive me back."

Christian answered her with a big grin.

They walked around the van to the trunk.

"Stand back please," he cautioned and waited for her to take a few steps back before unhooking the latch—which was basically a metal cord wrapped around the locking mechanism—and popping open the back.

Olivia saw the bright yellow luggage sitting on a spare tyre and reached for it.

"Don't worry, I won't let anyone else will snatch it from you," he said and smiled, but she gave him a cold stare and dragged her luggage over to the front.

"How do you open the doors?" she asked after a few futile attempts to open the passenger door. She didn't wait for his response and tried the large side door behind it; it rattled open.

"She is like a delicate woman; you need to know how to touch—" Christian stopped mid-sentence. "Practice, I mean," he finished the sentence with a big, embarrassed smile. Normally, Olivia would have laughed the comment away, but, after the day she'd had, she wasn't quite ready for that. She gave him a cold, blank stare.

Christian put her yellow luggage on one of the empty seats, and they got in and drove away from the airport. Olivia spent the next few minutes fumbling with the seatbelt. Each time she pulled it out, it'd either get stuck halfway or suddenly retract.

"Don't worry, the police won't stop us for that," Christian said.

Olivia glanced at him and wrinkled her nostrils when a cloud of smoke wafted through the window crack and into her face.

"I'm not worried about the police; I'm more worried for my safety. I feel like this van is going to fall apart any . . ." She stopped when she noted a distant, pained look on his face. *Not that long ago, you were scrambling to pay the bills too,* she reminded herself. There was no point in making him feel bad. *Besides,* she thought, *none of this was really his fault.*

Looking out the window, at the long stretches of highway and the tall buildings in the distance, Olivia felt a strange sense of longing. She still had her right hand clasped on the seatbelt, holding it more out of assurance than anything else. Small cars drove past as the van moved along at a steady pace—steady enough to send in much-needed fresh air to blow out the exhaust. Huge signboards displayed words she couldn't understand, but she saw something which looked like "airport" on one of them.

Gazing into the distance, Olivia wondered if her mother had ever travelled the very highway they were on. While watching a truck with a picture of cattle on it, she wondered if there was something here for her, something deeper than delivering a fair share of the Rusu fortune to the rightful heirs, something more connected to her.

A voice invaded her thoughts, and she glanced over at Christian, who was staring at her with a smile on his face. Had he asked her a question?

"I'm sorry?" she said.

"I said, I bet your flight was smoother than this, huh?" he joked. As he shifted gears, the van creaked and bounced for a few seconds before steadying itself. She smiled at him.

"We don't have to talk now," he said with the same neat smile he'd been flashing all day. "But it's a five-hour drive; might as well kill some time."

Olivia nodded and moved her eyes to the dashboard. There was an old stereo latched on it with a few wires sticking out. She wondered if that worked. Christian seemed to have followed her gaze and shook his head.

"Hasn't worked in months. But you lucked out. I'm a tour guide by profession so I'm used to talking all through the drive."

"I bet," she said, letting the awkward moment stretch.

"I mean, we can just sit in silence for a bit if you need to digest that incident."

"I'm just tired," Olivia excused herself. She didn't want to be rude. After all, it was the thoughts about her mother, not the earlier misunderstanding, that were causing her silence now.

Christian nodded, still smiling. "Of course."

The van turned off the highway three hours later, leaving the tall buildings behind and ushering them into a whole different scenery, one not unlike the pictures Olivia had seen on the internet when she'd looked up Romania before travelling. She sat up, having been leaning against the window the whole time, and gaped at the splashes of green and yellow out her window, like paint on a canvas. They were surrounded by farmlands and mountain roads. In the distance, the setting sun added soft oranges and reds to the scene. For a moment, Olivia wasn't bothered by the occasional bounce or sputter of the van.

"It's beautiful, my Romania, huh?" Christian said. They hadn't spoken much in the past three hours, except for Christian's occasional "sorry about that" when they hit a bump. "Turbulence," he'd say.

Olivia no longer felt as emotional as she'd been at the beginning of this ride; the silent drive and the beautiful scenery had softened her mood. She'd taken long journeys like this with her mother. It had been so long ago, she couldn't remember the destination, but she could still remember the bus with its people in it—reading books, leaning against the windows, or sleeping. She could also remember staring at the forests, at the trees twirling past them. The memories had always felt like a dream, but in this moment, she felt that dream come alive again.

"Yes, it is beautiful," she finally answered Christian.

He smiled, looking relieved. "We have a lot of fresh green land and mountains spreading across the horizon. It's like a painting."

Olivia nodded. "A very pretty painting."

"Do you like art?" he asked, slowing down to take a short bend, avoiding a branch stretched out across the road.

"I do. Not the boring ones of fruit."

"Or empty dishes someone left behind after a meal," he joked.

She laughed. "Or those. I like landscape paintings. And anything with people in them."

"Yeah, me too. Especially crowds from the past. Makes me feel like I'm time travelling."

"Yes, me too. I love those!"

She glanced at him. His eyes were on the road, so she watched him for a moment; the smile on his face and the way his fingers moved on the wheel, his arms bulging through his shirt. She looked away when he turned toward her. He reminded her of those guys she read about in books, the handsome rich types. *Except, in this case, I'm the* ... she paused halfway into that thought and frowned. The whole idea of inheriting the Rusu fortune and coming here hit her fresh again, turned everything surreal again.

"I'm really in Romania," she muttered to herself, but it came out a little too loud.

"What's that?"

She looked at him. When their eyes met, she shifted her gaze to the cracked windshield.

"I still can't believe I'm in Romania."

He smiled and nodded. "I know that feeling. Not that I've travelled out of the country, but I used to feel that way when I first came to the city from the village. It felt like a dream; like there was a whole world out there calling out to me."

It was getting dark outside now, so he turned on the headlights, which flickered briefly before stabilizing. Olivia watched a truck drive past, the first they'd seen since turning off the highway and onto the smaller roads.

"Not a lot of cars out here," she said after the red backlights of the truck grew smaller in the rear mirror.

"It depends on the season, but in late fall like this, not really. A few cars now and then, but mostly locals, or farm trucks heading to the village. You get the occasional tourist buses at the right time of year, but those are rare."

"It's funny," she said.

"What is?" he asked, glancing at her and then back at the road. The headlights pierced through the thickening darkness, illuminating the flickering bodies of insects.

"I can't help but feel like all this seems familiar."

"You mean you've been here before?" he asked.

She shook her head.

"Oh yeah, I remember. You said this is your first time here."

"But, somehow, it still feels familiar."

He pursed his lips, tilting his head an inch or two. "Well, you have family here, don't you? Elena?"

Olivia stopped herself from shaking her head—maybe Elena had told him that they were related. She shrugged. "Or maybe it just reminds me of some countryside I've seen back home in America."

"Or that too."

A shimmering moon had risen, sparkling stars popping up around it. She stared at the sky for a while, drawn to the mysterious beauty.

"What is America like?" Christian asked.

She tilted her head. "Well, it's not much different. Some parts look like this here."

Christian scoffed.

She frowned at him. "What's that for?"

He answered with a shrug. "That's the most American response."

"Oh really?"

They hit a cluster of rocks and the van bounced for a few seconds.

"Mm-hmm," he replied. "Most Americans, at least the ones I've met, tend to think the world isn't that much different from home."

"And isn't that right?" Olivia joked.

"Maybe, maybe not. My money's on maybe not." He turned and looked at her. "Don't get me wrong, I think America is fascinating, but I also think the world tends to look different the farther away from home you get."

Olivia nodded slowly and smiled. "You're quite good, you know?"

She could almost *hear* his smile. "That's a pretty ambiguous compliment. Good at what?"

"It's not a compliment, more of an observation. I mean, your English is quite good. So are those conversational skills you claimed earlier."

"I'm glad we've found something to agree on."

She laughed. "Although, so far, your bus is not on par with your service. At least it hasn't run us off a cliff yet, so that's good."

She shuddered and rubbed her palms together.

"Does the heat work?" she asked and reached for one of the knobs. "It's freezing." Her eyes went to Christian, who turned to her. His eyes popped when he saw her touching the knob.

"Wait, don't—" he tried to warn her, but was too late. The knob popped out and rolled under the seat. "It doesn't work," he said.

"I can see that," Olivia countered.

"But she's pretty reliable and sturdy," he commented and tapped the dashboard. "I mean my van. She might be old and rusty, but she's got a lot of fighting spirit and . . ."

Before he could finish his sentence, the van croaked and the engine stalled, guttering as it shook down the road until it slowed to a stop.

"Come on, come on," Christian begged and turned the key, pumping the pedal as sweat lined his forehead. "Not now. Come milady. Start already."

Olivia looked bewildered and pinched the edge of her seat, suddenly aware of the silent darkness around them. And the even darker woods.

Suddenly, the headlights flashed, and the engine squeezed out a few hopeful puffs. "Ha!" Christian let out an excited scream, but it was premature; the van bucked and hissed and died down almost instantly.

Christian clicked his tongue when thick smoke floated out of the hood.

"Uh oh," he muttered.

"Uh oh?" Olivia asked nervously. "But the van's been smoking all day."

"Yeah," he answered and scratched the back of his head. "But that's the bad kind."

He pushed open the door and stepped out, shaking his head. Olivia rubbed her arms and followed him out of the van. The hood was emitting enough heat to cook an egg.

"I can't believe this." Olivia rolled her eyes.

Christian, who'd been staring at the hood, looked up and nodded. "Me neither. She's usually reliable."

"Doesn't seem reliable right now," she scoffed. Her head ached. A firefly drifted past her face.

The hood creaked as Christian tried to open it up, wincing and shaking the heat from his fingers as he did. Olivia paced back and forth, rubbing her arms as she tried to remain calm. *A warm bed would be nice right now*, she thought and remembered her old apartment—not the mansion.

"It's an easy fix," he announced as he stared into the hood. Then he shook his head.

"Doesn't look like it," Olivia said. "And it's not reassuring when you keep shaking your head that way."

Something crawled over her foot and she squealed and jumped forward—right into Christian, who caught her before she could fall over. She instantly felt the warmth of his touch around her waist and arm, could smell his scent of fresh soap.

"Easy, ma'am. I'll be in much bigger trouble if something worse happens to you."

Breathing in short gasps, Olivia pushed away and tumbled back a step. "I'm fine. I think a snake just crawled over my foot."

"I don't think a snake would crawl over your foot right now, with all the noise—"

"Can you fix it?"

"Well . . ." He looked at her with regret.

"You just said it's an easy fix."

"Oh, yeah. And it is." Christian sucked in his breath. Olivia felt a tightness in her chest. "It's an easy fix . . . if I can get the parts."

Olivia's looked at the back end of the van.

"No, I don't have the parts inside."

Shivering from the cold, she rolled her eyes and threw her hands up. *Perfect.* She was stranded in the middle of nowhere in a creepy forest with a dead van and a total stranger—except, there was something about this total stranger that made her feel not so terrified. In fact, somehow, she felt safe with him. *Maybe it's his pretty smile.*

"There's nothing to be afraid of," Christian said, staring at her.

She looked away and sighed. "So now what? Do we call for help?"

He looked down the road. "Towing services are closed at this hour, but the closest town is only an hour away, on foot. Would have been faster in my van."

Olivia was tempted to make a saucy remark, but she was far too terrified of the creepy sounds around her—the insistent croaking and groaning of whatever exotic bugs or worse were hiding in the bushes. Olivia took a step closer to the road, away from the pitch-black shadows of the trees. Farther down the road, she thought she could see lights.

"I wouldn't call it a town, actually; it's more like a small village—not that I can really tell you the difference," Christian was saying.

The lights were growing brighter. It was definitely a car. She started waving her hands in the air like flags.

"Oh well, so if we . . ." Christian stopped and looked at her, a puzzled frown on his face. "What are you doing?"

Olivia kept waving her hands in the air. She felt a twinge of hope as Christian turned toward the two dots in the distance.

"Oh!" he said. The car drew closer and, as if they were a couple of invisible ghosts, drove past without even a honk.

Christian shook his head.

Olivia threw up her arms in frustration. "What the . . . Why didn't he stop?"

"Well, for a start, you're driving down a dark lonely road and you see two strangers by an old van, and one of them waving like a lunatic."

She flashed him a quick look and he winked before continuing.

"Would you stop?"

Glancing at the flickering headlights and the stretch of dark road, she realized they might look like a couple of suspicious individuals. Of course people would think it was a trick to rob them. Less than a few hours ago, she too had been almost robbed at the airport, so she shut her mouth without giving him an answer.

"Besides, it could have been a *she* in there, you know," he said in mock offense. He was probably trying to make her laugh. She gave a sad little chuckle before sighing deeply.

"It's getting really cold."

"I have a blanket," he said and went around the van. He pulled out her luggage and opened the front door and fiddled with something behind the wheel until the headlights went off. Then he produced that blanket from one of the back seats and grabbed the yellow luggage, which balanced easily in his left hand.

"We have two options." He handed her the thick, wool blanket. She threw it over her shoulders. It felt rough and heavy against her neck.

"One, we stay in the van overnight."

Olivia narrowed her eyes as he smiled, gesturing for her to hold on.

"Option two, we walk to the next village. It's an hour down the road."

"Why can't you go into town while I wait?"

"I can't leave you out here alone at night in the dark."

She glanced at the black shadows of the woods. Did something move? She shivered and nodded in agreement.

"I guess we'll have to walk into town then."

"As you wish, Miss Carter."

She looked up and felt that skip in her chest again when she saw him staring at her.

"Well let's get going already." She reached for her luggage.

"Don't worry, I've got this." He flashed her a smile, but she remained emotionless and turned around. Christian shrugged and followed her, bag in hand.

The rocks crunched under their feet as they started their walk along the road toward the small village. Olivia buried her chin into the scratchy blanket when a draft of cold wind blew across her face. From behind her, she could practically feel Christian watching her. She turned around to look at him and saw him taking off his jacket.

"You seem cold," he said and offered her the jacket.

"I'm fine. I have the blanket."

"You sure?"

"I can manage, trust me."

He nodded and put his jacket back on. She could tell he was holding back from insisting. She thought about wrapping his jacket around her, having his scent on her body. *No, I definitely don't need that.*

Olivia took out her phone and tapped on the Maps icon. The connection wasn't strong; it took the application forever to load.

"Not enough faith in your guide? I know where we are." Christian said.

"Just curious about the area, that's all."

"I *am* a tour guide, you know. Answering questions about the area is literally my job."

"Fine." She closed the map but turned on her phone's flashlight. "Tell me about this place."

"With pleasure." His eagerness seemed genuine. "There's actually a lot of history in this area."

"Is that so?"

"Yup, very much so. As a matter of fact, we're not too far from Transylvania, our destination."

"Oh, that's the place with the vampires, right?"

Christian gave her a dissatisfied frown. "You make it sound so ordinary. No, it's not 'the place with the vampires.'" He made air quotes and scoffed. "That's where Dracula's legend was born. That's where his castle is, where it all began."

"Oh, that." Olivia watched as Christian's face melted at her flat response. It made her oddly giddy. Any revenge for today, no matter how small and indirect, was satisfying.

He cocked his head to the side and added, "Most tourists aren't this . . . underwhelmed by Dracula's castle."

Well, most tourists don't get their bags stolen at the airport or stranded in the middle of nowhere in the dark. She had to bite her tongue in order to keep those words from spilling from her lips.

"What can I say? I've never really been into horror stories."

"Oh really? Well, I've got a spooky story for you," Christian responded, a sinister smile on his face.

"What part of not liking those stories did you not get?"

"Trust me, my story is interesting, and it's a great way to pass the time while we walk. It's like they say: two's company and an hour-long foot trek feels like ten minutes."

"Huh?" Olivia mumbled.

He chuckled. "You get the idea."

"The idea that my so-called guide is trying to confuse me? Yeah, I do." She shooed away an insect flitting over the tip of her phone. "Go ahead," she said. "Tell me your spooky story."

"I thought you didn't want to hear it?" he asked.

"You convinced me with that whole two's company thing, so go ahead."

"Alright then. There was once a young farmer who lived in an old village of stone houses in the hills. He was said to be the first man to settle in those hills. He cleared a patch of land, felled some trees, and built himself a nice house."

"Sounds . . . quaint," Olivia said.

"Anyway, he got married and lived up there with his wife for years. They never had any children, although they tried, but they were quite happy. He was a successful farmer, too, with cattle and chickens and fresh produce. Some said he was blessed, others said he had to be using some sinister power or something." He turned to her. "That's what happens when you're successful: people get jealous."

She nodded.

"Anyway," he continued, "one day, many years later, the farmer was riding in a cart with his wife, taking their fresh produce to the village as they always did, when they got attacked by robbers. His wife was dragged out of the cart while the man was held down and made to watch as they killed her. They say his screams shook the trees and pulled the spirits of the woods. The man killed himself right there, next to his wife, and their bodies were taken by the forest, their blood mixed together in the earth."

Olivia shuddered, then pulled the blanket tighter around her shoulders as if it were the cold.

"The spirit of the man is said to roam through these woods, thirsty for blood and vengeance. They say that when you pass through this area at certain hours, especially when the night is still, you can hear his cries."

Olivia listened to the scraping of their feet on the ground. She slowed her steps to walk closer to Christian.

"I think I can almost hear the cries," he whispered. "We must be close to where it happened."

"Stop it!" She hit his arm.

They moved in the small halo of light cast by Olivia's phone. The moon hung low in the sky, making the shadows of the trees and tall grass pop.

Suddenly, a wolf howled in the distance and almost immediately after that, there was a cracking noise from the bushes. She gasped again as she jumped into Christian, shuddering and burying her face into his shoulder. The forest grew still once more. She opened her eyes when she realized Christian's arm was on her lower back and his muscular chest was heaving from laughter. Clearing her throat, she pulled away and flipped her hair. Her cheeks burned fiery red as she looked away in embarrassment.

"I wasn't scared, just a little jumpy," she muttered in a last attempt to salvage the situation.

He gave her a disbelieving look, a teasing smile on his face. "You literally jumped into my arms."

Her cheeks burned even hotter and she lowered her gaze.

"As I said . . . just a bit jumpy," she repeated.

"There's nothing wrong with being scared. Fear makes us human, and strength is born from fear."

"I said I wasn't scared," she snapped. He froze, his smile gone. The words had come out colder than she'd wanted. "I'm sorry. It's been a long day."

"It's all right. And you know what, we're in luck. Look over there." He pointed ahead. Olivia looked in the direction he was pointing and saw dots in the distance—lights.

"The village." She sighed and closed her eyes, her thumping heart easing. "But will they help us?" she wondered, a newfound doubt creeping into her mind.

"Of course they will," Christian said. "This is Romania."

She thought of the woman who had stolen her luggage and the car that had passed them not too long ago. But she didn't say anything. She looked over at him as he stepped closer.

"I think this just flew off when you uh . . . were a bit jumpy." He waved her shoe at her.

"Oh." Her eyes went down to her white sock. She hadn't even noticed. "Thanks." Their hands grazed when she reached for the shoe. She felt that skip in her chest again and blushed, nearly dropping the shoe. "Thanks," she muttered again as they walked together down the road, this time in silence. Somewhere, an owl called out to the cold night wind.

***

It took them another twenty minutes to get to the village. Small farmhouses lined the road, pushing inward. Dim lights hung from poles and buildings. A dog barked somewhere in the distance, but otherwise the place was peaceful, an idyllic country setting with cattle and chickens and that smell of fresh hay and the night breeze.

"It's a village," Olivia said.

"I know." Christian tilted his head.

"No, I mean, you said I'd be the judge if it's a village or a town."

He nodded in recollection. "Yeah, I did say that." He switched the luggage to his other hand. "Over there," he said and pointed at a red brick building with white grout lines that looked stained and aged. Flowerpots lined the outside with cute little blue and yellow flowers growing out of them. Water dripped along the edge of the roof and the windows gave off a soft, flickering orange glow.

Christian knocked, and a moment later an old man wearing dark wool pants and a blue, long-sleeved shirt answered. The man looked at them and his boxy chin pulled back into a kind smile. His white hair was combed over to cover bald spots. The two men exchanged words in Romanian.

"He asked us to come in," Christian translated. Olivia nodded and smiled back at him. The old man turned and walked into the house, ushering them in, but Christian grabbed Olivia by her arm, holding her back.

"The people in this town, this man and his wife included, are very religious," he said. Olivia pinched her lips.

"I forgot my rosary beads at home," she joked, but Christian let go of her arm and scratched the back of his head.

"Emm . . . what I mean is, they think we're, well . . ."

Olivia shook her head. "That we're what?"

"That we're married."

"Oooooh," Olivia whispered. "I see."

"It would be better to play along. To simplify things for old-fashioned souls, if you know what I mean. If they think us improper, they might turn us away."

Olivia nodded and threw Christian one last embarrassed look. "Yes, I get it."

"Well then, after you, *dear*," Christian whispered with a teasing look on his face. Olivia went into the house with a fake grin to keep up the charade.

The warmth was very much welcome. The inside of the house reminded Olivia of an old American farmhouse—something from the '30s. Everything was wooden, and a few of the walls had purple-striped wallpaper on them.

They were brought into a small living room filled with stacks of broken radios and old TVs. The man gestured at them to sit down on the green sofa behind a wooden coffee table. Christian and Olivia sat down.

"Ana," the old man called out to his wife and then said something in Romanian to her when she entered the room. Then he turned to them, still beaming with that calm smile. "Make yourselves comfortable. I'll sell you the part you need by morning," he suddenly said in broken English.

"The morning?" Olivia repeated and exchanged looks with Christian who quickly cut in.

"Uhm, we'll need to be getting back tonight. No use staying till morning." Then he added a few more words in Romanian.

Olivia nodded in agreement, but the old man shook his head, speaking to Christian in Romanian. Olivia watched, glued to both of their lips.

"What did he say?" she asked when there was a break in their conversation.

"He says we'll have to stay the night, rest and have dinner, and that he'll sell me the part tomorrow morning."

"Why not tonight?"

Just then, his wife Ana came in with a tray holding two steaming cups. She was wearing a pink flower-patterned long-sleeved dress with her silver hair pulled back into a braid. She had blue eyes and a warm demeanour.

"Ah, sweet Ana," the old man said, smiling at her like they were newlyweds. Olivia picked up a cup from the tray and smiled back at the woman, Ana, who returned her smile before offering Christian the second cup of tea.

The old man then spoke to Ana in Romanian. Olivia watched, almost bemused, as the woman set down the tray and dramatically clasped her chest, her face full of surprise. Then she turned to Olivia.

"Dangerous," was all Ana said. Olivia couldn't help but notice the look of genuine worry on the woman's face.

"Dangerous?" Olivia turned to Christian. He frowned.

"Apparently, the bears in the forest have mated early this season. He said they're aggressive," Christian said. "They attacked a farmer after dark last week on the same road we just walked on."

"Oh," Olivia mumbled.

"We have a room. It's empty," the old man said. "It used to be for our son, but he lives in Bucharest now," he added with a soft smile at Ana. "She misses him."

Olivia couldn't help but think it cute the way this old couple was with each other. Even all the money in the world, which she basically had, couldn't give her that. She opened her mouth to ask about a hotel, but the old man added in a strong accent:

"You will stay the night. Come, I'll show you where."

There was no room for arguing. The old man led the way down a small corridor by the kitchen. Olivia raised her brows at Christian, who shrugged as if it was no longer in his hands.

The wooden bedroom door creaked as the old man pushed it open. Ana came up behind them and walked in first.

"I keep tidy for my son," she said in broken English and with a wistful sigh. The room was simple, with a desk, bed, red curtains, and a large wooden dresser. Olivia's gaze froze on the tiny bed next to the small wooden desk. Even if they had been married and allowed to share a bed, how on earth did Ana think they'd both be able to fit? Lying on top of each other? She turned around, her eyes wide at Christian, who smiled and said something to the old man and Ana before closing the door behind them.

Olivia crossed her arms; Christian avoided her gaze. They stood in the room, silent for a while until, finally, Christian exhaled and walked over to the small window. He looked up at the sky. "Beautiful night."

Olivia ignored it. She was more focused on the whole sleeping-in-a-tiny-room-with-a-stranger thing. Although, after everything they'd been through so far, he almost didn't seem like a stranger anymore.

She looked from the bed back to Christian, who was watching her intently.

"I know what you're thinking," he said, and his eyes moved slowly to the bed. Olivia opened her mouth to speak but shut it.

"You don't have to worry. Of course we won't sleep in it together."

She looked at him. "I'm not worried."

He raised an eyebrow at her. "Yeah? Your lip is twitching and"—he looked down at her waist—"if you clench those fists any harder, I'm pretty sure your knuckles will pop."

She looked down at her hands, surprised to see that he was right. She released her fists and gave him a *What now?* look.

"I'll sleep on the floor, and in the morning I'll fix the van." He grabbed one of the two pillows from the bed. She stepped quickly out of his way then felt stupid. It wasn't like he was going to pounce on her. Was he?

"We should get some rest," Olivia suggested. She quickly moved over to the bed and placed a hand on it. The soft blanket made her realize just how tired she was. She wanted to dive into it. She sat on the bed, feeling the slight depression of her weight against the mattress. All she wanted now was to take off her clothes and sleep for a few hours, but she doubted she could relax—let alone take off her clothes—with Christian in the room.

She took off her shoes, stretched out on the bed, and sighed again—actually, it was more of a groan mixed with relief. Her aching legs relaxed against the soft bed. For a moment, she was completely preoccupied by the relief of resting her body on a comfortable bed in a warm home—but her attention came back when Christian moved over to the wall by the door. He turned the lights off, and Olivia blinked, feeling nervous all over again.

Her heart skipped when she heard the familiar jangling of a belt. She sat up, definitely tense now.

"W-what are you doing?"

"Just taking off my pants. I have boxers on, and I can't sleep with—"

"Please don't!" The jangling stopped, followed by a slight ruffle.

"Yes, ma'am."

"Thank you," she thanked him, still sitting up.

He mumbled a few quick words in Romanian. Her eyes remained on his dark figure as he moved through the room to a spot on the floor a good distance away from the bed—which wasn't that far, honestly.

She lay back on the bed, trying to relax. There was no way he could have slept on this bed, she thought to herself as she moved her hand just a few inches to the side and touched the hard wooden frame. *Definitely not.*

Except for the creaking of the old wooden house, the room was silent. *He's still awake,* Olivia thought to herself as she listened to his slow breaths.

"I'm sorry about today," he said. She heard a slight ruffle and imagined him stirring on the floor. "I'm sure if I had a website for my tour guide services, you'd probably give me one star. Or maybe two, if I'm lucky."

"Maybe two and a half, at most," Olivia said, and he chuckled.

"I wouldn't want to read the review," he said.

"Yeah? Why not? You think I'd be brutal?"

"Mm-hmm. If I'm going to get two and a half stars, I might as well do what I want tomorrow," he said in a teasing voice, and they both laughed.

The laughter died down after a few seconds, and the silence kicked in again. She waited for him to speak, squirming slightly on the bed.

"What about your family? Why did you come alone?" he asked.

My family. She closed her eyes and sighed.

"Dead. In heaven, maybe. I don't know. But yeah, they're dead. My parents died in a car accident."

"That's terrible," Christian said. "I'm sorry, Olivia. I truly am."

She pinched the blanket, feeling the warm, soft fabric between her fingers. "It's been years now; I still miss them, but I manage pretty well."

"Death is . . . well, it's one of the craziest anomalies in the word."

"Philosopher mode, huh?" she said trying to lift the mood. She hated it when people pitied her. "But yes, nature is flawed."

"I have my moments," he added with a chuckle. "I lost my dad too, and now I dread the day I'll lose my mom as well." His voice was low now, serious. "I know you shouldn't think about things like that, but it's hard to just push away the thought if you've already seen a loved one go."

"I'm sorry to hear that. So, it's only you and your mom now?" Olivia asked, lifting her head and squinting through the mass of black in order to see him.

"No, I have sisters. Four beautiful sisters."

She could practically feel the joy in his voice. It was charming. "Four! Wow."

"Yeah. My mom and dad loved each other a lot. Literally," he joked.

Olivia felt the heat rush into her cheeks.

"Carter," Christian said.

"Hmm?" she mumbled.

"That's an American name, right? Carter."

"Yes. My mom was Romanian, and my dad was American."

"I see. How do you know the Rusus? Elena said you're distant relatives."

Olivia felt the urge to tell him about the whole inheritance stuff, but then, maybe Elena had a reason to say they were distant relatives. Maybe to protect her from someone who might scam an American tourist with no ties to Romania.

"It's complicated," was her response. "I guess that's what I'm here to find out. Do you know anything about my mom's family? Her name was Maria Balan. She must have known the Rusus."

"Balan? Never heard of it, but families move away to the bigger cities all the time. Like magic. Poof. Gone overnight, leaving nothing behind but empty old farmhouses."

"Oh," Olivia said absentmindedly.

"But I can ask my mother. She's lived here her whole life. She might know something."

What if his mother knew hers? Had stories to tell about her? Olivia felt a warm glow inside her. "Thanks. That would be very kind."

"Sure thing. I think we should get some rest now."

"Yes. Who knows what will happen tomorrow," she said. "I might have to take another star off your rating."

"Or maybe I'll earn one back," he answered, and she chuckled.

CHAPTER SEVEN

O livia opened her eyes for a minute and closed them again, dipping in and out of sleep. She could still feel the blurry flashes of her fading dream as she slowly woke up. The bed creaked softly as she stirred awake. Another minute went by before her eyes fully opened and she took in the small room. It looked unfamiliar—the walls and the curtains and the small window. Then everything from last night came back to her: the van breaking down, the long walk through the woods at the side of the road, the nice old couple, and . . . *Christian!*

She jolted upright, the bed creaking, and bent over to look at where he lay.

The floor was bare; not even the sheets he'd used were still there. Her fists tightened and she bit her lower lip.

"He left," she said and shuddered. *My luggage! What if he stole that? What if he abandoned me here?*

She jumped out of bed and rushed out the door. Then the voices hit her. Low, peaceful conversations in Romanian, punctuated by the occasional laugh.

She stopped short at the doorway when she saw Christian settled down on a chair in the kitchen, his arms bare and resting on the table. He was saying something in Romanian to Ana when his eyes shifted to Olivia, and his lips spread into a wide smile. He gestured for her to come over.

"Good morning," Christian greeted as Ana looked up. Her eyes brightened when she saw Olivia, like a grandmother pleasantly surprised at the appearance of her favorite grandchild.

Olivia smiled and looked at the table being set. She felt a rumble in her stomach when she saw the food—a loaf of thick-sliced bread, cold cuts, yogurt, fresh cucumbers, and tomatoes.

"It looks delicious," Olivia said. It looked great, the way the brown, green, red, and white blended together to create the picture of a perfect breakfast.

Christian reached for a slice of bread. "It tastes delicious too."

The old woman set a bowl down and went over to attend to a steaming kettle. "I get coffee," she announced.

"Take a seat; you slept heavily and snored loudly, like the bears in the forests," Christian said with a grin.

"I did not snore," Olivia responded.

"My bad. Of course you didn't," he said and looked up when the old man walked in.

"Sit," Christian repeated, and she hesitantly approached the chair beside him.

The old man greeted them and settled into the chair opposite them. His wife sat beside him and, after a rather long prayer, started to serve breakfast.

"You had a good night, no? Bed not too small?" the old man asked. Olivia blushed and looked down at her plate, wondering where to start.

Her mother had rarely made Romanian meals or done anything relating to Romanian culture in general. It was almost as if her mother wanted to forget something—ban Romanian life forever.

She looked at Christian, hoping he could tell she was embarrassed by the couple's insistent stares. Luckily, Christian took over that conversation. "She fell asleep as soon as she hit the bed." He laughed.

"Yes. Snore very loud," the old woman said with an innocent smile, much to Christian's amusement.

"Have coffee," Ana offered and poured from a ceramic pot. Olivia saw that curious smirk on Christian's face as he chewed slowly and watched her. Olivia muttered her thanks and took a sip from the cup. It was strong. The taste hit her hard, and she puffed her cheeks and held her chest, coughing as soon as she gulped it. Her eyes moved around the table. The family laughed while she coughed and let the coffee settle down her throat, leaving its bitter tanginess slapping the insides of her cheeks.

"Turkish coffee, the strongest around," Christian chimed in and she felt like pinching the smirk off his face.

"Maybe too strong for you?" the old man asked.

Trying to prove them wrong, she took the cup to her lips and pounded it. Her cheeks flushed and her eyes watered as she tried her best to hold back the cough rising through her throat. She gulped and smiled. "Not at all."

"Don't have more, you'll get dizzy," Christian whispered, lifting his hand as if he wanted to touch her arm. Olivia raised her chin, trying to hide her embarrassment.

"More please," she said, and Ana obeyed.

The cold cuts tasted delicious. She closed her eyes while she chewed the meat, savoring the taste. She looked up. The old man was smiling at them. He'd asked a question, but it hadn't been in English, so Olivia looked to Christian.

"They want to know how long we've been married," he said.

Olivia dropped her fork and lowered her voice. "Can't we just tell them the truth?"   Christian, his face cool, nodded. "Fine, I'll just tell them the truth."

She smiled at the old man.

Christian continued, whispering to her, "I'll tell them that we're not married, and that we only met yesterday and slept together in their house. In the same room, I'll add. And they'll assume in the same bed—"

"Two years," she said, exasperated. She held up two fingers at the couple. "Married two years."

Christian grinned. "Thanks, *honey.*"

The couple nodded and smiled at Olivia and Christian.

After breakfast, Christian and Olivia thanked the nice couple and left the house. It was a beautiful morning; bright clouds and the warm sun hung over the stone floors and colorful plants. Olivia saw the van parked in front of the house.

She glanced at Christian. "It's fixed?"

He nodded.

"How?"

He shrugged and smiled as if he enjoyed the look of wonder on her face. "Fixed her this morning. When you were still happily snoring away."

Olivia checked her wristwatch with a raised brow. "It's only eight now," she said incredulously.

"I couldn't sleep." He shrugged his shoulders again and opened the door to the van, which creaked loudly. The van shook as he climbed into it.

Turning around, he added, "It was very hot in the room with my sweater and pants."

"It was freezing out," Olivia countered and tried to open the door from her side. The handle snapped stiffly without budging.

"I'll get it." Christian grabbed the handle from the inside and the door swung noisily open. She climbed in and Christian looked at her.

"I have to admit I'm not used to sleeping in a room with a beautiful woman."

Olivia blushed and looked away, holding back a smile. When had she last heard someone use the word *beautiful* in the same sentence as her name? It made her fluttery on the inside. Then she looked at Christian and frowned.

"You're probably teasing me again."

"I'm not teasing you," he argued.

"Well, I don't believe you."

"You don't believe me about the teasing or the fact that I'm not used to sleeping with a beautiful woman in the same room?"

Olivia waited a few seconds before answering. "Both."

The wires sparked as soon as Christian clipped them together, and the van started, the engine coughing.

Christian gave her one more lingering look before turning the steering wheel and driving down the road. Olivia wanted him to say something else; she wanted to hear that word, *beautiful*, again, but he stayed silent, and so did she.

***

The whole airport incident was slipping further back in her mind with each hour Olivia spent with Christian. During the drive, he was lighthearted and carefree, joking and laughing in a way that she couldn't help laughing along. But there was also this far-off look he'd get when the conversation lulled and he drove in silence, his gaze fixed on the road ahead. During those times, Olivia found herself staring at him, the cracked window blowing his scent in her direction. She wondered what was going through his head.

He turned to her at one point while she stared and their eyes met. Too late to look away, she smiled at him. He smiled back. Her stomach tightened with that tingly feeling again.

"Wanna hear a joke?"

"Sure," she answered almost too eagerly.

He smiled. "Okay, here it goes."

"I'm listening."

"Why did the Romanian stop reading?"

She was smiling already.

"Why?"

"They wanted to give the Bucharest. Ha!"

It was a terrible joke, and yet, Olivia burst out laughing.

"Get it?" he asked.

"I got it. Yeah, because the capital is Bucharest and it sounds like . . ." She laughed again. "Oh man, that was bad."

Christian chuckled. "Don't say that. It's one of my best." He turned to look at her. "Hey, I wanted to ask your permission to stop by the store first and then at my house? I have to get some things for my family. They rely on me and I didn't make it home last night."

"Yeah, sure that's fine. I already texted Elena about the whole incident."

Olivia sat in the van while he made the quick stop at the store—a small brick building with vegetable baskets in front of it. He came out with two bags and a grateful smile on his face. Looking at the bags of food that had to be for his family, Olivia couldn't help wondering what his life was like at home with his mother and four sisters.

"Thanks," he said when he climbed back into the van and started it. By now, the loud, sputtering engine seemed almost normal to Olivia.

"It's fine. Really."

He nodded and adjusted the bags on the back seat. Olivia saw the green and purple of vegetables, a block of cheese, some milk, and meat.

When they arrived at his place, Olivia immediately recognized it as a farmhouse.

"It'll take only a minute," Christian said and stepped out of the car. He reached for the bags in the back and grabbed them. An onion bulb rolled out, and Olivia caught it, following him out of the van.

"Here," she said and offered him the onion. He was about to open the bag to let it drop in when a woman came out from the house. She walked slowly, almost like she was limping. She was incredibly pretty, and there was a glow in her eyes when she saw Christian. Onion still in hand, Olivia watched as Christian went over to the woman and hugged her tight. A little girl squeezed out from between the hug as if emerging from a secret door and jumped on Christian. The woman looked slightly older than him, but not much.

"He has a wife?" she muttered to herself in disbelief. Of course he does. She could totally imagine a gorgeous young man like him being snatched up by a beautiful older woman.

The little girl's playful voice mixed with Christian's as he spoke to them in Romanian, all the while not glancing once in Olivia's direction.

Olivia's eyes moved away from them and fixed on the onion in her hand. She felt scandalized. He'd never mentioned a wife. He'd been so willing to pretend that they were married. To sleep in the same room. And all that *beautiful woman* nonsense! She felt like an idiot.

She squeezed the onion until the smell became stronger. She let it drop before her feet and wiped her hand against her coat.

I'm never seeing that man again, she vowed to herself, her fingers sticky and reeking of onion. She got back into the van and waited, feeling more irritated with each passing second. He returned some three minutes later, smile still on his face.

"Hope I wasn't gone too long." He jumped into the van. Without giving him as much as a glance, Olivia scoffed and looked out her window.

Christian was silent for few more seconds; she could feel his eyes on her. Then he started the van. "Off we go."

"Good," Olivia mumbled, still glancing out the window. "Let's get this tour over with."

***

They arrived at their destination after fifteen minutes of silence. Olivia had stared out the window the entire time, brushed off all of his attempts at conversation.

When they stopped again, it was in front of another little farm; except this one was rundown and needed repairs everywhere—broken sheds, cracked walls, moldy windowsills. It was shocking!

How could Andrei Rusu let his sister rot away like this? At least now, with her share of the inheritance, she'll be able to buy whatever house she wants, Olivia thought. Why would a billionaire have family living in a heart-breaking situation like this one, and still will away all his money to a total stranger? It was even more puzzling now than when Mr. Stanley had announced it the first time.

An older woman waited outside the small house. She was thin with thick lines under her eyes. She was wearing a knee-length faux leopard coat. Another woman, much younger and dressed in pink pants and shirt, came out to join the woman as the van rolled to a stop.

The ladies walked up to the van and waited for Olivia to get out, all smiles.

"You must be Olivia," the older one said, her English thick with a Romanian accent. She squeezed Olivia tight, then broke the hug but held on to her hand. "I am Elena," she introduced herself, flashing her teeth in a broad smile. She turned to the other, younger lady. "And this is my daughter, Alina."

"So good to meet you," Alina said, her accent also seeping into her words. She grinned even wider than her mother as she came in for her own embrace.

"Thank you so much for this warm welcome." Olivia gave them a genuine smile, enjoying their kindness. She flashed a scornful gaze at Christian, who frowned.

Then Alina went over to Christian and hugged him. She kept her arms around him as she asked, "Why don't you ever text me back, huh? Too many girlfriends, I think."

And he tried to add me to that list as well.

Christian tried to squirm his way free from Alina while awkwardly chuckling. "Alina, you know I'm always busy."

Reluctantly, she let him go. He turned to Olivia, but she looked away.

"Come on in," Elena said and led Olivia into the small house. The banged-up wooden door groaned as it opened, looking like it was going to fall off its rusty hinges any moment.

Elena must have noticed her gazing at the door. "We're trying to manage," she said, her sad eyes on Olivia. Then her gaze wandered over to Christian, who was still by the van.

"What are you doing?" Elena asked. Olivia turned around to see Christian taking her yellow suitcase out of the van. Christian, just like Olivia, looked confused.

"I'm taking her suitcase out of the van," he answered. But Elena shook her head.

"No, no," she started and walked out the door, which groaned even louder this time. Olivia followed her, careful not to touch the door.

"You don't expect her to stay here, do you?" she asked, pointing at the house. Christian and Olivia exchanged puzzled looks. "I would never ask Olivia to stay in a poor house with a broken roof and mold creeping up the walls." She glanced at Olivia with wide, dramatic eyes. "Coming all the way from America only to stay in this tiny shed my daughter and I barely manage to survive in."

"I really don't mind," Olivia said. She had slept in a tiny room her whole life—well, most of it—and would never dare to complain. It wasn't as if she craved the luxury.

Elena put a hand to her chest as if having a heart attack. "No. I beg you, please don't argue with me. This is no place for you."

Olivia felt horrible. She didn't want to upset Elena anymore. She was probably embarrassed about her home. "I-I'm so sorry. I'll find a hotel nearby. It's really no big deal." She smiled at Elena, who sighed in relief.

Christian stepped closer, scratched his head. "I could drop her off at the Moto's Inn. It's clean, and Moto is well respected."

But Elena shook her head again. "That won't be necessary. We've already made arrangements. She will stay at Magura Castle."

Shock gripped Christian's face. "Magura Castle? Up on the mountain? *That* Magura Castle?"

Olivia had never heard of this castle, but judging by Christian's reaction, she got the distinct feeling that this day might not be much better that the last.

***

Christian couldn't shake the weird feeling that something was going on here. Magura Castle? That was crazy.

"What's Magura Castle?" Olivia asked. The confusion on her face reflected his own.

"Oh, it's been in the Rusu family for hundreds of years before it was lost to us," Elena said. "My dear brother Andrei himself bought it back for the family. Well . . . for himself that is, but let's go inside."

Olivia frowned. "Magura Castle, yes, I think I remember hearing that name during a meeting with my lawyer. Wasn't it being sold?"

Elena opened her mouth to speak when Alina chimed in. "It has not been sold yet, so, technically, the owner is still—" she was cut short when Elena lost her balance and stumbled sideways—right on Alina's foot. The girl yelped in pain.

"Oh, sorry dear, I'm not well today," Elena said. Christian folded his arms and watched them as Olivia stepped forward to offer a helping hand to Elena, who gladly accepted the offer and held on to Olivia's arm.

"I think I need to sit down," Elena said, throwing a pitiful look at Christian. "My old sick heart," she added, coughing. Then she turned to Olivia and smiled. "Come now, dear, there's coffee and cake for you inside. I just can't wait to get to know you. You must have a lot of questions about our family."

Olivia smiled and muttered a polite thanks, and they turned to face the door again.

That melodramatic sickness must have come overnight, Christian thought as he watched Elena limping into the house. Christian rolled his eyes and leaned against the van. It was all theater.

Alina stepped up next to him, and they exchanged glances.

"Mother at her best." She rolled her eyes. She made to come closer, but he quickly turned around and opened the van door, as if he had something important to do. When he turned around, Alina was stomping away.

At the doorway, he saw Olivia turn around and give him a polite, almost formal, smile.

"All the best with your tours," she said coldly. "Thank you for the . . . interesting ride."

"No, no," Elena said. "No need to say goodbye. He will wait for you outside." She paused as Christian and Olivia exchanged looks. "Our sweet Christian will be your driver to the castle," she said before going into another coughing fit, dramatically clutching her chest. "Isn't that so, Christian?" she asked, wheezing slightly.

"Well, we didn't really discuss the details but I guess—"

"There is nobody else I would trust my dear Olivia with," Elena said. "It is settled."

His eyes shifted from Elena to Olivia. Her face was drawn. She was clearly sick of him and his van. He felt his jaw clench, but he couldn't blame her. Either way, he'd do whatever Elena wanted. He needed the money, whether Olivia was sick of him or not.

"That's fine, I guess," Olivia muttered politely to Elena. She looked like she'd just eaten a lemon whole.

He watched them enter the house while he stood by the van, trying to piece out everything. Something seemed odd about the whole arrangement: the thing with the castle, and Elena suddenly playing the dying old lady.

He scratched the back of his head and walked around the van, running his fingers along the dents and scrapes on the vehicle.

"She's acting weird, even for Elena," he mumbled to himself and settled inside the van. He kept his eyes on the door and leaned back, folding his arms behind his head. Family heirloom or not, why send Olivia to Magura Castle? It was one of the scariest places in all Romania. Maybe there was something she wasn't telling him. Then again, it wasn't any of his business. But he couldn't help feeling that it all had something to do with the Rusu fortune. Somehow, Elena was trying to get more money. How rich was Olivia, anyway? He hadn't wondered about that until now.

"Not my problem," he said. Whatever was going on here, Olivia was strong enough to take care of herself. He could still picture her face at the airport when she was fighting for her bag, blocking his van with a look in her eyes that could kill. He smiled and shook his head. There was something unique about Olivia, some trait he'd never seen before. A hidden strength and honest kindness—even if the kindness wasn't directed at him.

The door opened and Alina came out. Christian straightened up and watched her come around to the driver's side.

"Good. You're still here," she said. She leaned closer to his side of the car.

"Yeah, I'm waiting for . . ." Christian was saying when she adjusted herself against the door, drawing down her top in the process. Alina was pretty, but as he cared for attributes such as kindness and intellect, of which she lacked both—not his type. He cleared his throat. "I guess I won't be needed for a while, huh?"

"That's what Mom sent me to tell you."

"Okay," he said with a sigh, reaching for the wheel. He gave Alina a curt nod and started the van. She stepped back, her arms crossed.

"I'll be back in a few hours."

He revved the engine, gave her a warm smile, then drove off.

Once again, he thought about Olivia. The family fortune. How were they related? Her last name was Carter, not Rusu. Her father was American and she said she'd never been to Romania before.

Maria Balan. She'd told him her mother's name had been Maria Balan.

His mom would know something about the Balans, he thought, turning the van onto the small, but buzzing, market road as he headed for home.

CHAPTER EIGHT

The scratching sound in the cracked ceiling above her could have been a rat scurrying over a broken wooden frame. But Olivia tried not to focus on that. The house seemed smaller and shabbier than she'd expected.

They sat around a wobbly table beside the kitchen and drank coffee. Olivia glanced at the colorful pile of clothes on the worn sofa. The house was run down, but there was no obvious mold or broken roof like Elena had mentioned. The pungent stench of cigarette smoke and thick perfume was hard to ignore, though.

"You will like some coffee," Elena said. Olivia smiled with a nod, hoping it wasn't as strong as what she'd had this morning. It had taken her an hour to get rid of that dizzy feeling. Alina made the coffee, setting the pot delicately on the table while she regarded Olivia. There was a book on the table, a thick text on biology and anatomy. Olivia picked it up just as Alina made to grab it.

"Is this yours?" she asked with a friendly smile, and Alina nodded. On closer observation, Olivia realized that Alina was actually quite beautiful. With a little less makeup, she'd be stunning. She had strangely elegant, long fingers and an appealing, confident smile.

"Anatomy?" Olivia flipped through the pages and saw notes crammed in the margins and large sections of text highlighted. It reminded her of her years in college.

"I would like to be a doctor someday," Alina said. Olivia could hear the pride in her voice. She smiled and handed Alina the textbook.

"I'm sure you'll make a great one."

Elena cleared her throat. "Universities are expensive. Not for people like us." She shook her head then smiled. "But let's have coffee." Elena let out another cough, covering her mouth as she did. Alina patted her hand and grimaced.

"Mother's health seems to be worsening each day."

"I'm so sorry about that," Olivia said.

"I will be fine." She took a deep breath to gather herself. "I just need some rest and things will be better."

She looked up at Olivia and took a sip of her coffee, carefully wiping her lips with the tip of her pinky. "We are grateful to have you, Olivia, really." She turned to Alina. "Ask Alina, she'll tell you how happy I was to receive your letter. It was like the very heavens opened up above us."

Alina nodded. "Mother almost fainted."

"Not almost," Elena chimed in, clearing her throat. She squeezed her daughter's hand. "I *did* faint. Remember? Right there, by the door. You said, 'Mother come and see this letter.' I didn't want to because I thought it was another bill." She shook her head and let out a sigh. "We have so many of those."

Olivia lifted her mug to her lips and inhaled the strong smell of coffee.

"But Alina promised this letter was different. So, I read the letter and there it was. You said you wanted to come to Romania and see us and give us a share of Andrei's fortune. Suddenly everything else went 'round and 'round in my head and next thing I knew, I was waking up in Alina's arms right there." She pointed to the door just beyond the cramped living room.

"I'm so sorry," Olivia said.

Alina looked from her mom to Olivia. "I have to be honest. I didn't think you would really come, but Mother never doubted you. You're like an angel, falling from the sky to save us. Even the smallest amount would help toward mother's medical bills."

Olivia squirmed in her chair, uncomfortable with the overwhelming amount of gratefulness. She didn't feel like a savior. She felt like a fraud.

"Alina, stop it. It doesn't matter how much, only that we were not forgotten," Elena said, gazing at Olivia.

"No, you were not forgotten," Olivia said. "I'll have to wait for Mr. Stanley, my lawyer, for the details, but soon we'll all sit down and things will change for you. I can promise you that much."

Elena grimaced for a second, then bit her lip. She looked like she was either holding back one of her coughs or, strangely, like she was angry. But then she smiled softly. "Of course, we understand."

Olivia knew this probably wasn't how they wanted things to go. Their house was literally falling apart around them, and Elena didn't sound like she was going to get better any time soon. Even Olivia was annoyed by this plan, but Mr. Stanley had been very clear with her before she left.

"You want to what?" his voice had raged through the phone. He was with her less than twenty minutes later, pacing around while she explained her intentions to him.

"It doesn't matter whether it seems right or not, Andrei did not will anything to his sister, and I'm sure he had his reasons." He stopped pacing. "I don't think you should go against that."

"Maybe," Olivia had replied calmly and stubbornly. "But I've already made up my mind, and past family feuds are not strong enough of an argument to me. So unless you have any real reasons, I'm leaving for Romania soon."

Mr. Stanley had let out a defeated sigh, massaged his temples, and said in a much-softened voice, "How much are you intending to give them?"

That had caused another argument. And yet, Olivia looked at the two women and felt deeply satisfied that she had defied Mr. Stanley. She did, however, agree to wait for details until he arrived in Romania and could oversee the transactions. Looking at the poor state the house was in, and also Elena's health, Olivia was sure he would finally agree with her decision.

"This is good coffee, thank you," Olivia said, not sure how long she'd been quiet. She hadn't even sipped it yet. The ladies smiled at her and thanked her furiously again. They were so kind. She wondered how she looked to them: some old flame's daughter, who'd taken money from these poor people when they needed it the most. It took everything in her to hold back the details she had in store for Elena and her daughter: *a majority of the Rusu fortune.*

She squeezed the mug and finally sipped the coffee. Strong, but not as strong as that Turkish stuff.

"Is something wrong, Olivia?" Elena asked with a look of worry on her face. Olivia placed the mug down and tried to smile. It wasn't convincing and she knew it. She couldn't hide the guilt from her face.

"I'm sorry," she said. Elena smiled.

"Sorry? What for?" Alina asked.

Running her finger over the tip of the mug, the black liquid rippling with the gentle motion, Olivia wrinkled her forehead and remained silent a moment longer.

"I'm sorry about this whole mess with the inheritance. I truly don't understand how Andrei would cut you out of the will like that. It doesn't make any sense."

Elena sighed heavily. "Well, don't blame yourself, dear. None of this is your fault. We are grateful you are here. We truly are."

Olivia wanted to ask what happened—how would one have a billionaire relative and somehow end up like this? The question burned on her tongue, but Elena dabbed her eyes with a crumpled pink handkerchief and looked like she would burst into tears.

"It's not your fault," she said, the hanky smeared with eyeliner. "It's a sad story," she sighed and lowered her gaze. "My brother and I . . . we had a huge fallout many years ago."

Alina reached for the small coffee pot and refilled Olivia's mug.

"Thanks," Olivia muttered.

Elena looked burdened for a moment but then nodded her head. "I think you deserve to know the truth and yet . . ."

"Truth? What truth?" Olivia wondered.

Elena nodded again. "The fallout I had with Andrei," she answered, her brows drawn together. "It was about your mother, Maria."

Olivia slid her hand off the warm body of the mug and stared at Elena.

"My . . . my mother?"

Olivia leaned closer, but Elena looked away, blinking rapidly as if she'd said too much.

Olivia exhaled, biting her lower lip as she felt her heart pound. Here she was, close to knowing something about her mother's secret past—even if it was just a tiny piece of the puzzle—and Elena was being hesitant for some reason.

"I'm begging you, Elena, I need to know this; it's very important to me, and everybody else who could tell me about her is dead. As I told you in my letter, I have nobody left." The crack in her was voice evident now. Elena looked at her daughter as if to consult her. Alina gave a short nod.

"All right, I'll tell you about it. The little I know."

Olivia smiled and wiped her eyes. *Gosh, was I already crying?*

"Andrei and your mother, Maria, were married when they were still young. That was a very long time ago, you see." She shook her head somberly. "The marriage, it wasn't a happy one. My brother was a troubled man when he was young. He treated your mother horribly. I don't want to go into details, let the dead rest in peace, but it was not a good time for your mother. By our Lord in heaven, I couldn't just stand by and watch beautiful Maria ruined by my brother"—she clenched her fist and slammed it on the table, her lips pursed—"even if Andrei was my own flesh and blood."

The silence hung thick in the air as Elena paused. Olivia held her breath, her head filled with images of her mother crying and the young Andrei hovering over her, yelling. Was the whole inheritance a way to make up for all that? Reparation for his younger self's sins?

"I confronted Andrei," Elena said with a hiss in her voice. "I told him to get a hold of himself, told him to stop being a fool. Not every day do you get to marry a woman like Maria Balan, pretty, selfless, kind . . . but he wouldn't listen. So I convinced her to leave and helped Maria escape to America. It was the best I could do for her." She focused on Olivia now. "Maria met a nice American man over there. She told me so herself in a letter, which Andrei burnt when he found it. He was furious!"

Dad, Olivia thought and felt a knot in her stomach.

"And they had a beautiful child." Elena smiled at Olivia.

The silence drifted in again. The ladies watched Olivia carefully as if expecting a response from her, but her eyes were cloudy and her face plain. She was thinking, speechless.

"That is all I know, my dear child. Over the years, Andrei became a better man, but he never forgave me for convincing Maria to leave. But that was the right thing to do, and I would rather die poor than have done anything different."

Alina kept her gaze lowered on the table the whole time her mother spoke, casting a quick glance at Olivia before resuming her blank stares.

Olivia bit her lower lip. *I wish Mom hadn't been so secretive about this whole thing; I wish she'd told me about her past.*

"I don't know why my mother never told me about all this," she said out loud.

"Women want to forget the demons of their past. Trust me, I know what I'm talking about," Elena said. She turned to Alina. "Her father was a drinker. We never speak of it."

Alina nodded quietly.

"I understand," Olivia said. "I still wish my mom had been open with me about all this. Everything feels so . . . strange and full of gaps." She sighed and looked around, then quickly settled her gaze back on the table before they would think she was scrutinizing the house. "If I could find a box labelled *answers,* I'd grab it with both hands." She said.

"I would too," Alina said. "With these badly-needing-a-manicure hands." Alina held up her hands with cracked, pink nail polish. Olivia giggled.

"Well, let's have some cake now and talk about other things, shall we?" Elena announced with a smile and pointed at a box on the kitchen countertop for Alina to grab.

"Sounds like a good idea." Olivia smiled, ready to change the subject, even though her thoughts were still clouded with memories and unanswered questions of the past.

After a long silence, they pushed past the topic of Olivia's mother and talked about various topics such as Romanian cuisine as time flew by. Or about how beautiful the countryside was.

It was already afternoon when they heard a loud, blaring honk outside.

"Christian!" Alina blurted as she ran outside. Olivia watched, amused, as Elena shook her head in disapproval.

"Young women . . . like dogs in heat these days," she said. "I think it's time." Elena glanced behind her at a cracked wall clock. "Look how the time has gone. It was so much fun having you around. Maria's flesh and blood. I cannot wait to see you again and continue where we left off."

See me again? Olivia tried to hide a frown. "Are you not coming up to the castle with me?"

Elena cleared her throat. "I'm sorry dear, but Alina has to take me to the doctor this afternoon. I don't want to be a bother to you, but would it be okay for you to go alone? Only for today? Christian will drive you."

Olivia lowered her eyes in disappointment. More time alone with Christian.

"I'm sorry. I'll go with you then," Elena said and coughed wildly, throwing her back against the chair and thrusting her chest forward. Olivia shot up from her chair and tried to reach for her, but Elena held out a hand.

"I'm okay, my dear. You're such a sweet child."

"Please don't worry about me. You have to see the doctor. I can go alone to the castle," Olivia said. "It'll be a lot of fun to check it out. I've never been in a castle before. A real one, I mean. Only seen them in the movies."

"Such a sweet child," Elena repeated. "I will come up there tomorrow."

"That would be great. If your health permits. Otherwise, I will just come back to see you here. No biggie."

***

Elena leaned against her daughter, holding the handkerchief to her face as the van rumbled off in a cloud of thick smoke. They waved eagerly and kept smiling until the van turned around a corner and disappeared out of sight. With a growl, Elena quickly straightened her spine and stretched out her arms, the knots in her joints popping.

"Now I may really need to see a doctor," Elena complained and rubbed her lower back. "My back hurts like hell." The grimace on her face turned to an excited smile. "That went better than I thought it would, even though you almost ruined things again," she said, turning to Alina. Her smile disappeared as soon as she noticed the sulky look on her daughter's face. "What's that look for?" Elena asked with a huff.

Alina sighed, still maintaining her drawn look.

"Talk to me now," Elena snapped with a sharp scowl on her face. Alina turned to her mother and muttered something.

"Your voice, Alina! Use your voice! You know I hate when you do that mumbling thing."

Alina sighed and folded her arms. "I think this is all too much," she answered as soon as the last words escaped her mother's mouth. "She seems really nice. I like her."

Elena clicked her tongue. "What did you say?"

Alina opened her mouth to respond.

"No, don't answer that," Elena said. "I don't care if you like her or not. Don't you get it? She's playing us as much as we're playing her. She came out of nowhere and stole what rightfully belongs to us. Why do I have to keep reminding you about that?"

"She doesn't seem to be pretending. I think she's being honest when she says she wants to help us."

With another irritated hiss and a wave, Elena shook her head in disappointment. "You're young . . . and stupid. I thought I raised you smarter, taught you about the world. I guess I failed you."

"Mother!" Alina said.

Elena rolled her eyes. "I can't believe you've been fooled by that act. What has gotten into you, Alina? Turn around, look at how we live. Do you really think a few thousand dollars will save us? Will that help you become a doctor? Wake up, will you!"

Alina mumbled something like a sulking child, but Elena could tell she was thinking it through.

Elena waited a moment for an answer, but when none came, she rolled her eyes and started walking away. Alina followed quickly. A sign that she was backing down—as always.

"I understand, Mom, I do. But maybe we can talk to her, make her see, and then we don't have to—"

Elena twirled around, her eyes wide and filled with irritation. Trembling with anger, Elena grabbed Alina by her arm and shook her. "Stupid! Sometimes I wonder," she said, her chest heaving. "Sometimes I wonder if you truly came out of my body, if you have truly suffered with me all these years." She let go of Alina.

Alina, cheeks flushed and eyes wet, rubbed her arms in silence.

"How can you be so childish? The Americans are selfish. She'll sit down with us and her lawyer, give us a few thousand dollars, and then feel like Mother Theresa herself, expecting us to fall to our knees before her." Moving closer to Alina, Elena sighed. "Is that what you want? To miss our only chance at making it out of here?"

Alina's lips shook and she started sobbing, her shoulders shaking as she closed her eyes to hold back the tears that seeped out anyway. Elena rolled her eyes and looked away. She swore under her breath but then softened her voice. "I'm only doing this for you, Alina. You're all I have left. What kind of a mother would I be wanting anything less than the best for her daughter? I have to protect you. That's my job."

Running a thumb over Alina's cheek, she rubbed off the thin trail of black eyeliner left by her tears. "I want you to go to school and fulfill your dream, be a doctor like you always wanted." She smiled. "Remember how you always came to my side with that rope around your neck, playing doctor? I'll never forget how happy you looked." Elena patted Alina's cheeks and looked away. "It's not like anything bad will happen to Olivia; I can promise you that. I just need her to see that she's not the rightful heir to the Rusu fortune." She gave Alina a quick glance. "With a little persuasion, of course," she said with a smirk. "A little scare, that's it."

Alina sniffed and wiped her eyes with the back of her hand. "I'm sorry, Mom. You're right."

Elena held out her arms and welcomed Alina into her embrace. "That's my girl." She pulled away. "Now go in and start cooking dinner while I take a walk to the market and get more cigarettes for us. It won't be long."

Alina nodded.

Elena watched with lips pressed tight until Alina had gone inside. Once the door shut, she rushed behind the small wooden shed next to the house and pulled out her cellphone, glancing left and right before punching in some numbers.

The line beeped a few times before it clicked as the connection was made. The cracking voice of an old man came through the other end with a stiff "Hello?"

Elena looked around once more, then whispered loudly, "They are on their way." That was all she said before she ended the call and let the phone slip back into her faux leopard coat's pocket. Her lips spread into a thin smile as she rushed onto the path that led into town.

CHAPTER NINE

Christian took another glance at Olivia as he drove down the small country road. Destination: Magura Castle.

Fused into a lovely blue sky, the sun cast blinding rays that reflected off the dirty windshield. It was one of those pretty late afternoons. He turned again to Olivia, tempted to ask if she was enjoying the view. Her gaze was distant, her eyes moving around the mountains and sky. Who wouldn't love this view? Green hills popped up in the distance, patched with yellow cornfields and brown farm sheds. In the backdrop, huge mountains formed a wall of blue spanning across the horizon.

Christian smiled. This was Romania, and it was his home. He turned to Olivia; the tour guide in him couldn't help himself. "It's beautiful, isn't it?"

They passed through groves of trees with orange leaves brushing in the wind. Dark green bushes lay farther ahead like clumps of broccoli stacked together by some organized giant.

Olivia mumbled a yes with a slight nod.

Didn't even bother to look at me. Christian focused back on the picturesque view, enchanted by nature's various colors: the blue splashed against the green and orange tones. It almost looked fake, like a beauti-ful painting had been spread across the windshield. It made him think of their destination, of how much of a contrast that would be.

He turned to her, wondering what she knew about Elena or the castle they were heading to. He played it all back in his head, the strange way Elena had behaved with her coughing fits. The display had reminded him of the TV dramas he'd watched with his mother. But Olivia hadn't seemed suspicious or worried at all. *It has to do with money, that has to be it,* Christian thought as he made a left turn, one hand clutching the gearshift. The thought disgusted him. Sneaking a glance at his passenger, he thought to himself, *What if I'm somehow part of this?*

"No," he muttered out loud by accident. Olivia turned toward him this time.

"What?"

"Oh nothing."

She nodded and resumed looking out the window.

I'm just a driver. I'm just doing my job: moving the client where I'm asked to. That doesn't make me a part of any of this. Olivia is a strong woman. She'll be just fine.

He rubbed the back of his neck, catching the dampness forming despite the cool breeze coming in through the windows.

You need the money, Christian, he reminded himself as he negoti-ated a pothole expertly, the van bouncing only slightly. His eyes went to the sun, which was partially hidden behind a thin cloud now, and then to the mountains in the distance and their faint white peaks. *It'll be winter soon. I need to fix the heat of the house before the cold hits. Yes, I need the money. I really do.*

He turned to see Olivia looking at him and forced a smile, but she kept her face blank.

"Were you able to get more information from you mother, on my family?" Olivia asked. Even though she was all business, Christian felt a slight surge of relief that she'd actually spoken to him.

"I thought you weren't going to speak a word till we reached the castle," he said with a smile. She ignored it, so he cleared his throat. "Sorry. I wasn't able to talk to her. My mother wasn't home."

She nodded.

They drove on for a minute or two before she spoke again, this time without taking her eyes off the road ahead.

"Tell me that story."

He turned to her. "Hmm, story? Which one?"

"The story about the castle. I feel like there is more to it. Why else make such a big deal of it in front of Elena's house."

He hesitated. If she was staying there, it wasn't a good idea to tell her about the castle's dark past. She must have noticed that hesitation because she fiddled with her wallet and pulled out one hundred euros, the green note crinkling nicely.

"This trip is already paid for," he stated. A cow turned to the right to look at their passing van, a bored look in its eyes as it chewed on some hay. Once again Christian found himself staring at the money. His sisters needed winter shoes, and this would cover them nicely.

"Come on, you're a tour guide. It's custom to give tips for good tours, isn't it?"

"Ugh!" he groaned and grabbed the money, tucking it away as Olivia stared at him, her eager eyes saying: *well you're bought now, so spill.*

"As I said, a long time ago, Magura Castle was once in the hands of a powerful Romanian noble family. Andrei Rusu's ancestors." He turned to her and found her staring back at him, hanging on his every word. "The thing is, the Rusu family fell into disgrace with Vlad the Impaler." He stressed the graveness of the word *Impaler*. Olivia cast a curious glance at him. "Apparently they dared what nobody else was brave, or foolish, enough to do and openly criticized him for his violence." He glanced at Olivia, his eyes set, "I don't think he liked being criticized openly, or even privately, I'm sure."

"The *Impaler*?" Olivia asked, drawing him back to that.

"Oh yeah, Vlad the Impaler. He was one of the most powerful rulers in the history of Romania. People identify him with Dracula, although he had nothing to do with vampires. Very controversial figure, though. He had Turks and other criminals impaled on wooden sticks. You know, hence the *Impaler* bit. That was his thing."

Christian saw Olivia shudder, a look of horror creeping onto her face.

"Anyways, one day, the little daughter of the Rusu family woke up to her entire family impaled in front of the castle."

"What the heck?" Olivia blurted out, her eyes wide and her mouth hanging open.

"I guess he *really* didn't like being criticized," Christian said with a shrug.

"That little girl," Olivia muttered, looking at the seat beside her as if the little girl was huddled up next to her. "Did he spare her because she was—"

"Too little to be impaled?" he cut in, his eyebrows raised.

She nodded.

"No. Not even close. Vlad killed countless Saxon children. It's like that thing people say: size don't matter."

Olivia shuddered again as he shifted the stick and stepped on the gas, jolting the van forward in a series of rattling lunges.

"He wanted her to be a constant reminder that the consequence for defying him was getting your whole family impaled."

"You make it sound so casual," Olivia said, her face flushed.

"I've probably just told the story too many times. Doesn't feel real anymore, you know?" This time his tone had a layer of seriousness.

"So how come Andrei had that castle if the family lost it?"

He adjusted the rear mirror then focused back on the story. "Andrei Rusu bought the castle back after he became rich. He was a superstitious man, had it cleansed by the church. He wanted to prove a point. That nobody, not even Vlad the Impaler, could curse his line. That they were glorious once more. Well, him at least."

Olivia shook her head and blinked slowly, rubbing her arm. "Cursed? Cleansed by the church?"

"Yeah, but it's nothing to worry about," he assured her. The wideness of her eyes and her pale face told him she was, in fact, worried about it. It probably didn't help that the lush greenery was gone and more clouds had cluttered the sky, creating a grim, dark horizon. The van rode up the mountain road, and with each meter of elevation, the darkness seemed to grow. No more dancing trees of green and yellow and orange, and no more marvelous hills. Instead, the scenery was replaced with spooky forests and rocky mountain patches.

"The castle, it's on top of the mountain?" Olivia frowned.

Christian nodded, watching as the lonely, narrow road cut through a dark forest, becoming steeper by the minute. Olivia squirmed in her seat, looking out at the crooked trees, dark and grey, branching out unevenly on either side.

"The Magura Forest," Christian explained.

"I don't see any houses or farms," Olivia said, looking around, probably hoping to spot even a single sign of life and color.

"You won't see any," Christian said. "The locals, well, they're terrified of these woods."

"Why?" Olivia asked.

As if on cue, a wolf howled in the distance.

"They're superstitious people. But it's more so the wildlife than the creepy trees and spooky history of this area."

Olivia crossed her arms. "Are you trying to make me feel better? Because it's not working."

He looked at her, narrowing his eyes. "It's the wildlife that scares them. I promise!"

She raised a brow. "Aaaaaand?"

He sighed. "And they think it's haunted and cursed." He let the words hang in the air for a few seconds.

"By . . ." Olivia said, waiting.

"By Vlad's ghost."

Olivia gasped and shot him a look. If there was any doubt about how creeped out she was, it was gone now. She looked like she'd spotted Vlad himself. She shifted a few inches away from the van's door, her hands clutched together.

"Vlad the . . ." She seemed unable to complete the sentence.

"The Impaler," he said, helpfully. "Not Vlad the Singer or, or Vlad the, I don't know, Negotiator, or the Peacemaker or even Vlad the Handsome," he joked, trying to brighten the mood. Olivia gave a small smile. *Good.* "I wonder if he was handsome. We can call him Vlad the

Handsome if you'd like. Give him the benefit of the doubt." He turned to Olivia, whose small smile was already growing stale as they drove.

Soon, the castle appeared in the distance, blanketed by dark clouds and thick, creeping fog.

"See, not so bad!" he said.

Olivia leaned forward, her forehead wrinkled high. "Is that . . . Is that the castle?"

Christian almost wanted to say something like "Oh no, not really, that's just another castle we'll have to pass to get to the actual Magura Castle, which is filled with cotton candy and puppy dogs." But, instead, he nodded, scratching his chin. "Yup, that's the castle. But it has its charms." As soon as he said it, a large group of crows cawed in the distance, circling high above the castle as if searching for something dead.

A terrified Olivia watched as the castle drew closer. The road leading up to the main gate was made of stone, grey and grim—just like everything else around it. The mountain behind the castle rose, dark and mysterious, along the horizon. Fog crept in from the surrounding woods, which were filled with bare trees lifting crooked branches.

The castle itself was enormous. Black roofs peaked at the top of thick, grey stone walls that had dotted square windows. The structure looked majestic and yet like something out of a medieval horror movie.

"This looks . . . creepy," Olivia said.

Christian chuckled. "Mm-hmm." They were approaching the main gate now—a huge, black construct of iron with pointy tips like pitchforks.

"Don't be creeped out by this place. None of those ghost stories are true. The castle is really interesting, and I should know."

"Because you're a tour guide, huh?" she asked, and he nodded.

She didn't seem too convinced. She rubbed her arms as they stopped by the main gate.

Suddenly, the front gate creaked and opened. Christian could tell that Olivia was holding her breath as she watched the moving spiked iron tips. The night was now sinking into blackness as the caws from those damn birds still raged in the distance like a soundtrack. A soft orange glow cut through the fog as a man holding a lantern approached through the open gate. Christian squinted. *Who the hell still uses lanterns these days?*

The man stopped right in front of the gate and raised the lantern, the bright orange glow lighting up the grim expression on his face. He was an old man, large and incredibly tall. His clothes could have been from any century, really. He was wearing brown leather boots and mud-stained cream pants. A dark wool coat with a hood covered the rest of his humongous body. Standing in the fog, with his face lit only by that dim light, he looked pale with rumpled skin folded by his deep frown. It seemed as if the face of an old man had been pulled out and stuck onto the shoulders of a muscular giant. The expressionless glare in his eyes made him look scary, Christian admitted. This was definitely not the small, friendly old keeper he remembered when he toured the castle last. He had never seen this giant before—he would remember a man like this!

"Relax," Christian said to Olivia when he heard a soft gasp escape her lips. He almost reached out to pat her hand, which was close to his, but he stopped himself.

The orange glow moved along the side of the van as the old man approached them, the lamp squeaking as it swung back and forth. Christian got out of the van and stepped in front of the man.

"Where is the old keeper?" Christian asked—in English. The man grunted and regarded Christian as if trying to determine whether he deserved an answer or not.

"Not here," the old man finally spoke in English, with a thick Romanian accent.

"Yeah . . . exactly. What happened to him?" Christian had to speak loudly over the humming of his van.

"He quit," the old man responded. "After the death of Andrei Rusu." He moved closer, his teeth bared as he spoke. "Said something about a curse. Superstitious old fool. I'm the new keeper of the castle. I'm Mihai."

Nodding, Christian looked at Olivia and then at the old man. "I'm supposed to drop the lady here off."

"I know," Mihai said, glancing at Olivia, who looked away immediately. He grinned and stepped aside, motioning them to continue.

Christian drove the van around the circular fountain, parking some distance to the main entrance. He glanced at Olivia again. She looked shaken, wide-eyed and silent, her fingers pinching the hem of her coat.

"That guy Mihai gives me the creeps," he said. Olivia nodded. He glanced at the side mirror, at the new keeper pushing the gates closed. The castle would be empty and silent. *How the hell is Olivia going to stay here alone?* he wondered and squeezed the wheel. He tried to push away whatever dreadful thought popped into his head about Mihai, and the weird way he looked at Olivia, but that was impossible. The old keeper had been his father's friend, was well known in town, but this guy . . .

Before exiting the van, Christian turned to Olivia with a smile. "Hey, would you like a little tour of the castle? I've been here before. Not many times, but the old keeper was a friend of my father's and let me tour the castle sometimes when Andrei Rusu was out of the country."

Olivia smiled back at him, her eyes bright with gratitude. "Yes!" she quickly answered. "That would be wonderful!"

CHAPTER TEN

C hristian could have been a mind reader for all she knew, but Olivia didn't care. When he offered to take her on a tour around the castle, she felt like throwing her arms around him. *Good thing I didn't,* she told herself as she got out of the van. *That would have been awkward.*

Olivia stayed close to the van and waited while Christian went over to talk to the keeper. *What was name?* she wondered. *Mi-something.* She'd been too preoccupied by the creepy feeling he gave her to bother with his name. But maybe she was just being judgmental. Obviously, whoever had hired him after the death of Andrei Rusu had confidence in him.

She watched Christian and the keeper talking from where she stood by the van and sighed with relief when Christian made his way back. The keeper disappeared into a small house attached to the outside wall of the castle, the yellow glow of his lamp trailing behind him.

"I told him not to bother about showing you around, that I could handle it," he said as soon as he got back to the van.

"Thank you."

He pulled out her luggage and shut the doors. "Just out of curiosity, did Elena mention anything about who Andrei left the castle to?" he asked, his eyes fixed on her.

Me.

Olivia stayed quiet. By now, she was certain that Christian didn't know about her inheritance, and she didn't want to tell him for some reason. Maybe she liked the fact that he treated her like a normal human being, which had become a rarity as of late.

Christian narrowed his eyes at her briefly, then grinned. "Anyways. It's a magnificent place. I'm sure you'll find the tour intriguing."

"Intriguing," she repeated under her breath. "Of course."

He walked around the van toward her, carrying her luggage casually over his shoulder as if it weighed nothing at all.

"Still terrified?" he asked coyly.

"No. Well, maybe a little uncomfortable."

Christian nodded. "It's a bit intimidating, this castle and its woods."

"I'll manage," she insisted, and he smiled.

"I guess we could put off the tour till tomorrow then."

She held her breath and her throat twitched.

He laughed. "Just kidding!"

"That's not funny," Olivia protested and turned around.

He followed her. "But it was."

She wasn't sure why she was leading the way, so she slowed down as soon as they got to the steps leading up to the main doors. She analyzed the gigantic wooden gates of the castle and let her gaze wander off to the dark sky and the sudden flashes of lightning.

Climbing the wide, grey stone steps to the castle's entrance, Christian turned around and announced: "I'm sure you'll be the girl that survives for the sequel."

She giggled and carefully climbed the first steps, peeking over her shoulder at the medieval looking courtyard. "This place is surreal." She took another step and looked up to see Christian already standing by the door.

"Let's make it fun, explore, shall we?"

She ran her hand over the human-sized lion statue next to the entrance gate. There were others like it towering on top of the massive walls—gargoyles. The statue felt cold and rough, and looked old. As a matter of fact, almost everything seemed ancient around here. She thought of the creepy vines crawling up the walls surrounding the castle she'd seen when they first drove in. They were dried up and brown with thorns sticking out, just like the ones in the Sleeping Beauty storybook she'd had as a little girl.

"Now brace yourself, my lady," he said dramatically as they reached the front door. He pushed the door and it creaked without budging.

She grinned. "Well that ruined the moment. I was expecting the door to fling open with rays of light shooting out, followed by the loud humming of an angelic chorus."

He turned around, smiling wide. "Me too! But now I look like an idiot. Let me redeem myself." He went down the steps, leaving Olivia alone.

"Please hurry!" she shouted after him. The main doors had those circular ring-like handles. She stepped up to the door and ran a finger over the cold iron handle, feeling the granulated bits of rust. A fresh breeze from the woods carried the smell of trees and soil. She grasped the locket around her neck, which held the picture of her parents.

"I'm in Romania, Mom. Hope you're okay with that."

"Okay, I'm back," Christian's voice boomed from behind her, and she quickly slipped the locket back into her top, exhaling as she turned around. He held up a bunch of keys. "Turns out Mihai must have forgotten to tell us that the door was locked."

"I think he did tell us when he growled a few times," she said with a chuckle.

"I thought it was more of a man-snort," he said.

"What?"

"You know, like when a guy keeps snorting the slime in his throat and . . ." He paused when he looked at her and saw what she was sure was a grimace on her face. He picked out a key. "Never mind. Let's get this party started. Now brace yourself for the best tour of your life," he said again, just as dramatically. And this time the lock clicked and the door creaked, and when he pushed, the gates opened wide.

"Wow," Olivia said with a gasp and he turned around.

"Damn right wow. No angelic chorus though."

"Or bright rays of golden light, but wow."

They stared at a long hallway lit up by torches—they were electric bulbs but still the real ancient deal. The walls were made of medieval rocks, lined with long, red rugs hanging several feet from the top. There were even armored suits standing alongside both walls, making it look like they were being greeted by rows of knights. Some were holding swords, other spiked weapons or spears. Olivia was breathless. This was insane! Like straight out of a medieval movie. And the craziest thing about all of it was . . . it was hers.

Christian led the way, and she followed. He was being the typical tour guide, walking slowly and pointing at this or that while he explained the history surrounding whatever he drew her attention to, including gigantic, golden-framed portraits of people she didn't know or an antique piece of furniture.

The air inside the castle was hot in places and cold in others, with a hint of that old carpet smell. There was something off about the space that she couldn't quite put her finger on. It wasn't uncomfortable inside or hard to breathe, yet it felt intense and uneasy like something was hovering around them, vibrating the air.

"You'll really like what's coming next," he said, leaving behind the library he had already elaborated on, a flashy grin on his face.

"Lead the way." She followed him past the sky-high wooden shelves filled with books. She looked over her shoulder once more to take in the massive fireplace in the library.

"You know what?" she asked and her voice echoed down the hallway they were walking down.

"Listen to that!" Christian said, pausing to listen to their echoing voices. "Nice acoustics." He turned around. "What were you saying?

"I was thinking with all those rooms, this castle could make a nice boarding school."

He nodded slowly as he eyed the place. "You know what? You're right. I never understood how one family alone would need so much space. Why not put it to good use?"

"Yes. Like in the movies, just not the horror ones."

"Great! Let's do it! Together!" he shouted, listening to his own echo. His brown eyes flashed in the dim light, and a strand of his brown hair fell into his pretty face. He looked stunning—as handsome as they came.

Olivia smiled, occupied with the thought of actually running a place like this with Christian. A warmth spread from her stomach throughout her whole body. For some reason, the idea was so wonderful it was almost painful. What was going on with her? Not only was this man taken, but she barely knew him!

They went through a door that led into the massive dining hall.

"This is where the family dined," Christian said, his voice echoing over the long dining table, above which hung burning candles in golden chandeliers. The place looked like it was waiting for its king and his knights to return any moment for a feast. "Isn't it wild," his voice interrupted the echoes of his last sentence, and Olivia turned to him. "Hundreds of years ago, people walked through this very hall we're standing in right now. The air probably smelling of roasted chicken and fine food, and there were probably a few children running between servants as they settled in for a luxurious dinner."

Olivia noticed the distant smile on his face and the way he looked around the hall. *He's really picturing it,* she thought to herself. Maybe he actually *could* see the children running around—she halted that terrifying thought right away.

"Must have been a pretty big family," she said aloud, still trying not to think about the ghost children.

"Pretty big," he said, motioning her to the table. "Most of these antiques have been preserved. Very well preserved, I'll say." He was holding a golden chalice that had been placed in the center of the table, its surface shimmering in his hands.

Olivia stepped carefully around the table, keeping Christian in her view the whole time, and ran a finger over the edge of the table.

"This reminds me of the Rusu mansion back in the States," she said and rubbed her fingers together. She had to hold back a cough as dust from her fingers rose into the air. "On a much smaller scale, I mean, and more modern than this castle of course."

"Less creepy and lonely too?" Christian asked.

"Yes, less creepy at least." She shook her head, hoping Christian hadn't noticed the sadness in her voice. With a smile, she held up one of the silver candelabras. Candles stuck out of its artfully decorated holders, glowing yellow and orange; she wondered if it was that old man, Mihai, who'd lit them. She turned the candelabra around so that she could see her reflection on its shimmering surface; it had a foggy tint to it, like frost on glass or the steam of someone's breath. She frowned and wiped the surface and her eyes caught something dull and white right behind her. She gasped and turned around sharply.

"What is it?" Christian asked, staring at her.

She narrowed her eyes and scanned the magnificent ceiling, the sweeping arches rising like waves. There was no one wearing a white gown, no floating ghost. She tried to stop the hammering in her chest as she turned back to the chalice to confirm what she'd seen. Nothing. Only her reflection. She placed the candelabra back on the table.

"Well come on," Christian said. "There's so much more creepy stuff to explore."

"Can't wait," Olivia said as she stepped close beside him. She took one last look behind her as they crossed the dining hall.

They went up red carpeted steps and down a long hall, which had so many rooms it would be impossible to explore them all tonight. Some of the rooms they did peek in were dusty and filled with cobwebs and old, covered furniture. And there was that same vibrating atmosphere in them.

"Do people still live in this castle?" she asked.

"Huh?" Christian said.

"I mean not now, but since Andrei bought it; did people stay here? I mean inside the castle. Andrei and his family?"

Christian scratched his stubbled chin. "You know, I'm not sure. The old keeper told me that Andrei rarely spent any time here, but I don't know if anybody else stayed here. To be honest, it's kinda weird that Elena asked you to stay here," he added.

It was weird, Olivia agreed. Why not a hotel or something. But then, it was her castle after all, so maybe Elena thought it would make Olivia feel better about the whole inheritance thing if she stayed here with Elena's approval—even encouragement.

"Maybe a little, but not as weird as you think," she responded, and they continued the tour.

They went over to the west wing of the castle. "I wish they had elevators in this place," Christian said. "Don't get me wrong, I love climbing beautiful stairs as much as the next tour guide, but come on."

"I should be the one complaining right now," Olivia said. "I'm the one who's supposed to stay here."

"Fair enough."

They were walking down the west wing hallway, their footsteps and voices echoing, when Olivia stopped, noticing that the portraits along this hall were all wrapped with heavy drapes, hiding the images beneath.

"I wonder what's under these portraits and why they're covered," Olivia said. Christian stepped over to one and touched the tip of the drape.

Olivia gasped. "Are we allowed to do that? Maybe we should ask Mihai first!" She could picture the old keeper scampering down the hall, muttering words she couldn't understand and waving that gigantic fist of his.

"Don't worry. Mihai doesn't own this place." He gripped the fabric and smirked. "Don't you?" He feigned a light tug, and Olivia held her breath, expecting the drape to fall off.

"Yes, but—" The words slipped her lips before she could stop them. She'd been so focused on the picture.

He let go and stared at her. Olivia felt as if she'd been caught with her hand in the cookie jar, but Christian turned as if nothing had happened.

"It's probably just pictures of old men hunting," he said and started walking slowly down the hall. "Like they usually have in castles. I wonder who first started that whole idea of lining pictures of hunting scenes, generation after generation and . . ." He paused and peeked over his shoulder, acting all innocent. Olivia still had her eyes fixed on the huge portrait, wondering why Christian had just tricked her into admitting that she did, in fact, own this place—or, more so, how he figured it out.

"Are you coming or are we just going to stand here all day? I can manage both. Well, maybe not." He looked out one of the tiny windows with iron bars into the darkness outside. "It's getting late, and I still need to show you the best part of this place." He walked up to her, a conspiratorial look on his face. "The dungeon."

That caught Olivia's attention. "A dungeon?"

"You have to see it to believe it," he said.

"God, not sure if I want to!" She laughed nervously.

Christian looked around, glancing from left to right as if he were lost.

"You do know where it is, don't you?" she asked.

"Of course I do. Sort of. Maybe."

She sighed.

"Don't look so disappointed yet, ma'am."

"Olivia," she corrected.

He cleared his throat. "It's like people say, the something-something is in the journey, not the destination."

She placed a hand on her hips. "The something-something?"

"I can't remember. But yes!" His eyes settled on a wooden, square sign on the wall. "Ah, here we are." He went over to it and Olivia joined him.

"It's some kind of map." He ran his hand through the engraved wood. "And . . . yes." He turned around quickly, bumping into her shoulder. "Oh sorry, didn't know you were so close behind me."

Olivia rubbed her shoulder, a warm tingle burning inside her. "It's fine. So do we know where the dungeon is now?"

He grinned. "Yes, we do."

He led her down the hall until they got to a door that opened to a winding stairway. The stairway was narrow and undecorated, like it hadn't been designed for the more distinguished members of the castle.

"These steps lead to the watchtower up there," he said. "There is no time today, but we can check it out another time. It would be nice to see the surrounding area from up top."

"Maybe."

He laughed. "Eager to see the dungeon, eh?" he asked and started down the stairs.

There was no proper response to that, so she remained silent as she followed him down the steps. The walls were dry and dusty; they left dark stains on her palm when she touched them. Something crept over her hand and she gasped, shaking it off.

"Something wrong?" Christian asked.

Her eyes went to the tiny black creature. She exhaled. "Just a spider."

144

The stairs led down to another narrow hallway, at the end of which was a metal door. It was locked. The rusted chains and lock looked ancient.

Christian scratched his head as he scanned the door. "No key. You'd think they would keep these places open. It's not like they still keep people down there." He turned to look at her, trying to hide a smile.

"Very funny," Olivia said as she noticed a key hanging on a large nail in the wall beside them. She took the key and reached for the rusted lock, slid the key in, and opened it. Christian joined her to push the heavy gates open.

They stared down into a winding darkness. No torches or creepy flames lined the wall, just the ominous silence as the last echo of the door's creak died.

"We could use our phones, or . . ." Christian walked over to one of the torches burning in the hallway and unhooked it, holding it high above his head. "Or we could use one of these fire hazards."

"Seriously, why does the keeper keep these torches lit?"

"I bet he does it to make this place creepier," Christian answered as they both stepped through the metal door. The flames from the torch crackled and wavered as Christian held it before them.

"You know what," he said, and she looked at him, "I think our modern torches will be much better down here."

"I think so too," she agreed and stared into the darkness in that short moment it took him to replace the torch and come back with the more familiar white glare of a phone's flashlight. Olivia's heart started racing. *I'm about to go down into a dungeon. A real dungeon!* she thought incredulously and wondered if she should take pictures. Mindy might want to see them. Oh and Mr. Right. She smiled at the thought of Mr. Right, but her mind was soon back on the dungeon, wondering what must have happened down there all those years ago.

"Much better," he said when he pointed the beam down the winding stairs. They moved silently, each step taking them lower and lower. They got to another gate—this time unlocked. Square metals with thick bars, not unlike the thin ones in modern jails.

"What if there's skeletons down here?" Olivia said. Christian halted and turned to her, his face serious.

"That . . . would be . . . awesome," he beamed.

There were no skeletons or dried-up bones, but the dungeon was impressive and terrifying at the same time, each room linking to the next, and the walls were filled with scratches and marks. A cold shiver ran down her spine when she realized that one of the marks was filled with dried blood.

"I think we better go back up," Olivia suggested inching closer to Christian, rubbing her arms.

"Had enough already?"

"Yes please. Don't get me wrong, it's all impressive but uh . . ."

"Yes, it's too real down here. I get it."

She nodded.

"Let's go back up. Too bad I didn't bring a good camera though," he said.

"Yes, too bad," she said without making any effort to hide her sarcasm.

When they got to the top of the staircase, Christian looked out the window again at the black night beyond. "Maybe we do some more touring some other time." He gave her a curious look like he was gauging her reaction.

A crow cried somewhere on the roof, and the wind howled against the windows. She shuddered and anxiously searched her memory for the most welcoming room of the tour.

"I think I'd like to go back to the library," she said recalling the crackling fire in the fireplace and the many harmless books. If she was to stay here by herself, it was there, and nowhere else, that she wanted to be.

"Your call, ma'am . . . I mean, Olivia."

***

The library was perhaps the most impressive of all the rooms they'd been in. It was huge, of course, with an enormous fireplace expelling comforting warmth with every crack and flicker of its flames. Olivia wanted to reach out to the neat stacks of books in the shelves and run her fingers over the pages and the antique covers. She felt like picking a book, snuggling by the fire, and disappearing into a different world.

"This place is beautiful," she muttered, running a hand carefully over the old leather spines of the books. "It even has that old-book smell," she said and sniffed. "But older!" As an avid reader, she felt like a child at a candy store. Christian joined her by the shelves and picked out a book, also taking a whiff.

"Yup, that old book smell," he agreed. "It reminds me of the books I read as a little boy."

"You like reading?" she asked, a book written in Latin open in her left hand.

He chuckled. "Of course. Where do you think I get all my excellent tour guide knowledge? I research and read whatever I can get my hands on." He ran his hand through his hair and smiled. "I uh, I have dreams of going to the university."

"I thought you already went . . ." She paused and tried to rearrange the words in her head. "You speak English so well."

"Thanks. But no, I'm still dreaming about going further than . . . this." He snapped the book shut and placed it back on the shelf, waving a storm of dust out of his face.

She said nothing else. *What am I even supposed to say anyway? That I understand what it's like to be confined to a small farmhouse? What it's like to struggle for food or money for heat in the winter?* Even before she inherited all this money, she never lacked any of those basic needs.

She continued to browse the books. Opening a few, she noticed cursive, almost illegible handwriting in some of the margins. It had to be Andrei's handwriting.

Suddenly Olivia heard footsteps outside the hall and froze. A long, thin shadow appeared in the doorway. Olivia gasped.

"What is it?" Christian asked and she pointed at the door, at the shadow rising through it. He frowned and walked over to it. She followed behind. They stepped out of the library and immediately saw Mihai walking up to them, mumbling something to himself.

"It was just Mihai. No need to be spooked," Christian said to her and she sighed. She still had a book in her hand and wanted to go back into the library to return it, but, staring into the library's open spaces and shadowed corners, she shuddered at the idea of going in there alone. She stretched her hand and placed the book on a stool by the door instead, muttering a low "sorry" to the book for not returning it properly.

Mihai now stopped in front of Christian and straightened his gigantic spine. He opened his mouth and said something, but she couldn't understand him. Was he speaking English? Eventually, Christian cut in.

She watched them talk for a while before the keeper took one unfriendly look at her and left. At least she thought he was leaving, but she soon noticed him following them.

"Let me show you to your room," Christian announced. "The keeper has prepared the former lady's master bedroom for you. I'm sure it'll be nice."

"Former lady, as in . . ."

"Long-time-ago former lady. Like medieval times. Andrei wasn't married, as far as I know."

Located on the second floor off the main hallway, the room was indeed nice—in a medieval way. The whole room was themed in red silk, including the wallpaper. A cozy fire burned in the corner of the room, which was filled with lots of dark antique wooden furniture. They stepped in, and Olivia's eyes fell on the huge bed. It looked like it had been taken from a movie set, with four posts and folds and folds of cozy-looking blankets. It was the type kings slept in.

"Nice, huh?" she heard Christian say.

"Very nice." She nodded.

He stood beside her. "I sure wish I could sleep in a room like this."

The keeper stepped into the room, and they turned around when he spoke. Once again, Olivia arched her eyebrows and glanced helplessly at Christian.

"He says the cook has left for the week."

"Oh," Olivia said, not even knowing this place had a cook.

"But the good news is the cook prepared several meals you can warm up in the kitchen."

The keeper nodded and mumbled something. He grinned, exposing a golden tooth. Olivia smiled back at him. Then he turned and left.

"So what do you think?" Christian asked, rubbing his hands.

Doing her best to ignore the creepy feeling still gripping her, Olivia smiled. "About what, the tour? Or the castle?"

"Both."

"The tour was great. Really in-depth and professional, I'd say."

He took a half bow and grinned. "And the castle?"

She sucked her teeth and bit her lip. "I think . . . it's great." A soft beep drew their attention to Christian's watch.

"Ooh," he winced and looked up. "It's getting quite late. I should be going now."

Olivia froze. "Can't you stay a little longer?" She glanced at him, then quickly looked away when their eyes met. "I mean, I could warm up something for you. It'd be boring having dinner alone."

"Tempting, but well . . ." He tilted his head from side to side and pursed his lips as if trying to weigh the offer. *What are you doing? He's married! Get a hold of yourself and be a big girl!*

"I'm sorry." Her eyes strayed past him and settled on Mihai, who was still lurking in the hallway. *What the heck is he doing there?* "I-I understand," she stuttered.

Christian turned around to the see what held her gaze captive, then turned back to face her. "On second thought, I am quite hungry. No harm done in taking in a quick bite before heading out, right?"

Olivia smiled with relief, a smile that faded slightly when she heard Mihai grunt in the distance before his shadow disappeared down the stairs.

"Great," Christian said, clapping his hands. "Let's go look for the kitchen."

***

The kitchen was built to serve a whole castle, with several modern cooking stoves and counters—the only entirely updated room in the whole castle. This could have easily been any other modern kitchen—for rich people, that is. The cook, whoever that was, had stuffed the fridge with different Romanian foods. After Olivia went through the plastic containers like a kid opening presents, she decided on Jumari, which was smoked bacon and greaves, and a Romanian soup with freshly baked bread on the side. Christian had also grabbed a bottle of wine and had displayed great acrobatic skills in carrying all the items from the kitchen to the dining hall in one trip.

They sat next to each other at the large wooden dining table, which felt weird considering all the other empty seats. The table had been set up for a banquet fit for a king and queen, and yet there was nobody but the two of them.

"I wonder how, back then, families had discussions over a long table like this."

Christian pointed at the chair at the far end of the table. "I bet the guy sitting all the way over there wouldn't have heard a thing."

Olivia laughed. Christian looked at her with a grin, his pretty smile warming her. Suddenly she felt guilty. *What about his wife?*

"Please apologize to your wife for me for making you late. I understand that you have to leave soon. They must be already waiting."

"My . . .wife?" Christian seemed confused. "I'm not married."

"The woman at your house wasn't your wife?"

"No, that was my mother, and that other cutie was my sister. One of them."

Olivia felt as if a huge rock had been pushed off her chest. But why did she feel that way? *It's not like I was jealous or anything*, she told herself. Yet, she let out an embarrassing laugh, feeling her cheeks flushing with more than just the wine.

"I'm so sorry," she said.

He waved off the apology. "It's an honest mistake." He sipped the glass of wine by his side then offered to refill Olivia's glass. She agreed.

"My mother married young, at seventeen, and I came shortly after that."

"Gosh, she looks amazing for a mom of five." She watched his arm as he held the bottle over her cup and filled it. This could have easily been a date with some prospective man who was romantically involved with her—only it wasn't. Christian was getting paid for driving her around, and this dinner was more an act of kindness than the beginning of a romance novel.

She slipped out of her thoughts and found him staring at her. "What?"

"I was only wondering..." He shifted in his seat, still looking at her. "I don't know if it's stepping out of bounds or anything, please tell me if it is, but I had a question."

Olivia glanced up at him. "Go ahead."

"It's probably not a big deal or anything, just wanted to know if you had anybody back home in America."

Olivia let a moment pass before giving him her response. It was kind of embarrassing. "There's no one back there, especially not a man."

He nodded, smiling. Olivia couldn't tell if it was a smile of relief or not.

"What about you? Any Romanian beauty waiting for you after your tours?"

"Nope. Only my mother and my sisters."

"You're lucky," she said with a sad smile. "I wish I had four sisters."

"No you don't, believe me. Last month when I came home, I found all my belongings scattered throughout the whole house. I started gathering them only to find myself attacked by four little monsters yelling I was ruining their scavenger hunt. Apparently, they used my stuff as clues."

Olivia laughed. "As I said, you are lucky."

"I am."

Suddenly, Christian looked out the window and sighed.

"What's wrong?"

He eyed his watch. "I'm so sorry, but I have to go now. It's already getting dark." He took out his phone and cursed under his breath. "Dammit. No cell service."

She also checked her phone. "Mine too, no service." She waved her phone at him. He frowned.

Footsteps echoed through the castle, and they both looked up. Olivia stifled a yelp when, out of nowhere, Mihai was suddenly standing by the table, leaning forward with his hands behind his back. A strand of white hair fell over his face, making him look somehow menacing.

"I think you better be going now," he said in a heavy, but understandable, accent, his yellow eyes fixed on Christian. "It's late outside and soon the thick fog will set. Dangerous for a drive, I tell you."

Olivia shuddered while looking at the keeper. His lanky shadow, which stretched out behind him, was thin and bent. It could have easily been mistaken for any of those crooked trees they'd seen on the drive up here. She tried to be open-minded, non-judgmental, but the thought of staying alone in the castle with that man made her squirm. And yet, Christian had a mother and several sisters to take care of.

"You should go, I'll be fine," she said. Christian exchanged looks with her, and then with Mihai, then nodded.

"I'll be back tomorrow with Elena," he said and started walking toward the hallway.

"Here, I'll see you out."

***

The darkness of the night was split by the headlights of the humming van. Christian was sitting behind the wheel, his gaze fixed on the wide-open entrance door of the castle—but more specifically, on Olivia and Mihai, who were standing in front of the door waiting for him to leave. The hallway's warm, soft glow highlighted both of their figures. His van was vibrating and spitting smoke, ready to roll down the small forest road to the village. His eyes narrowed, zooming in on Mihai. The gigantic keeper was two heads taller than Olivia; it looked like David and Goliath standing in silence next to one another. Why was he even out there waiting for him to leave?

There is something about this guy, something I don't like.

From the entrance, Olivia suddenly smiled, as if she had read his thoughts and wanted to tell him, *It's all good, I'll see you in the morning.* But was it all good? He felt a distinct heaviness in his chest at the thought that something could happen to her.

You're being ridiculous; she'll be fine.

Now Mihai smiled too, his yellow teeth exposing an ugly grin.

There is definitely something about this guy . . .

Christian sighed and turned the van off. The headlights died and the loud coughing engine was silenced, making way to the whistling the wind and the hooting of an owl somewhere in the forest. He got out and walked up to Olivia and Mihai. Olivia smiled and opened her mouth to say something, but Mihai cut in.

"Is there a problem?" he growled, crossing his arms. Christian stepped closer, right in front of him.

"I was just thinking it might be better to leave tomorrow morning. What if my old van breaks down again?"

Olivia's face lit up. "Yes, of course! You should stay here tonight," she offered. "Better safe than sorry. There's, like, a million rooms you could stay in. What's the harm?"

Christian looked up at the old keeper. "My van may be reliable, but she's pretty old after all."

"And don't forget the bears," Olivia chipped in.

"Yes, with their cubs and all." He looked from Olivia back to the keeper. "They're pretty aggressive. Mothers, right?"

At this point, he wasn't sure if they were trying to convince themselves or Mihai, but it didn't matter.

"Hmph," the keeper grunted and walked over to his small house without saying another word.

"What's eating Grandpa?" Christian muttered with a grin and Olivia shrugged, her cheeks flushed.

"I think we still have wine in our glasses."

"A terrible mistake that should be remedied right away," Christian smiled and passed her, entering the castle's hallways again.

Olivia followed, and together, with Mihai absent, they pushed the humongous wooden entry gates closed.

***

They spent hours together in the library talking about random things: God and the world, the moon and the stars, why cheap pizza was better than pasta—or not. Olivia had the most amazing time, laughing so hard sometimes her stomach hurt.

After a long yawn escaped her mouth, they decided it was time to say goodnight. They left the library and walked to the floor that held her lady's master bedroom. Christian had chosen the room across from hers.

"Well, this is goodnight then, Ms. Olivia," he said, walking her to her door. "It was pretty fun, huh?"

She nodded, feeling her cheeks blush. It almost felt like the end of a date. Except this wasn't a date. Christian was only being nice by staying with her. She felt guilty letting him stay, but when she'd been standing outside in the cold to say goodbye to Christian, listening to the giant next to her breathing louder than the howling winds, she couldn't help but feel terrified. So, yeah, she was more than happy that Christian was here—even if this wasn't a date.

"I had a lot of fun," she said.

"Yeah, me too, although I still insist that pasta is better than pizza."

"No way," she grinned. Then there was an awkward silence in which both exchanged shy looks and glanced away. For second it seemed as if he leaned in a bit, but it might have just been her imagining things.

"Well, goodnight," she said.

He cleared his throat and started walking. "See you tomorrow."

Olivia watched him for a moment then went into her room and slowly closed the door without fully shutting it. She could hear Christian's footsteps in the hallway as he walked to his room, followed by the slow whine of his door and the click when he shut it. She shut hers at that point as well, heading straight to the huge bed, which swallowed her up as soon as she dropped on it. A few moments later, she was sound asleep.

***

When Olivia opened her eyes again it was midnight—at least if the tall grandfather clock across from her bed was right. A small bedside lamp was on, casting a warm glow over her. She blinked slowly and sat up. She needed to go to the bathroom. Her eyes scanned the room wall to wall. There was no bathroom attached to it.

There's a bathroom near the kitchen, she thought, rubbing her eyes. But the thought of walking downstairs alone didn't sound appealing at all. What if that creepy keeper was ghosting around in the dark? She immediately thought about Christian and the fact that he wasn't far away. *Maybe I could text him.* She was reaching for her phone when she realized she didn't have his number, nor did she have reception.

Pushing aside the blankets, a soft sigh escaping her lips, she pressed her feet down on the warm Persian rug and walked, a bit of a stagger in her steps, till she got to the door. She opened it and peeked out. The hallway was lit by a dim wall light with a single flame that was so still it looked fake. Her gaze froze on one of the metal knights holding a sword. She half expected it to turn and start walking toward her. But it stayed stone still . . .thank God.

Telling herself to be a big girl, she straightened up once out in the hall, walking past scary-looking portraits and closed wooden doors. The castle resonated with a humming silence, which made her shudder, goose bumps spreading across her arms. She stopped in front of Christian's door. She knocked. Nothing.

"Oh for Christ's sake!" Bouncing on her feet—partly from her need to use the bathroom and partly from her need to get out of the hallway—she bit her lip, knocked once more, waited, glanced from left to right, then opened his door and walked into his room.

"Emm . . . Christian?" she whispered as she slowly walked over to the bed, a four-poster like hers, from which came his low, steady breathing. She froze.

Christian was splayed on the bed, dressed only in boxers. His right leg was bent with only a fraction of his thigh covered with the blanket. Everything else was exposed to her gaze. Her eyes settled cautiously on his chest, spotting the curls of hairs here and there and the squareness of his muscles. Feeling like a creep, her gaze wandered farther down to the smooth plane of his abs—and then there were his thighs, lined and curved and well-built. She gulped, her heart speeding in her chest the more she stared.

He suddenly gasped and shot up, his eyes wide open as he stared at Olivia.

"I-I am sorry!" She stumbled backwards and quickly jerked around, her cheeks burning a deep red.

"I felt someone looking at me," he said in a sleepy voice. "I'm just glad it's wasn't Mihai."

She folded her arms. "I-I just came to ask you to come to, well, the—the bathroom with me. Downstairs, I mean."

She heard the soft thud as his feet touched the ground, and the ruffle of clothing. "Pretty sure I won't be of much use in there with you." There was laughter in his voice.

She sighed. "Forget about it."

He laughed and stepped beside her, straightening his shirt over his torso.

"I'm already up, might as well come with you and save you from the ghosts."

She hated how childlike she must seem to him, but she nodded anyway. "Thank you."

She walked back out into the spooky hallway, and he followed her. The castle was quiet except for the howling winds in the distance of the night, which seemed to be getting stronger. Christian whistled and it echoed.

"Why are you whistling?" she whispered.

He shrugged. "Why are you whispering?"

"And since we're asking questions, I wonder why the bathrooms aren't, you know, inside the rooms too."

"It's an old castle. Believe it or not, they didn't have running water in those days, or the luxury of having a bathroom so close. Back then they used pots. Were there none next to your bed?"

Olivia tried to remember. "I don't think so, but maybe on the—" His laughter cut her off. She let out a little growl and gave him a soft smack on his arm.

"Very funny." She rolled her eyes.

"I know."

Once safely inside the bathroom, Olivia could hear Christian whistling just outside the door. Her socked feet rested against the cold, white tiles as she relieved herself, her pink undies and pants bunched down around her ankles. Her eyes moved from the square tiles to the stained porcelain sink that was dripping. This bathroom was nothing like the rest of the castle. It was old, sure, but it had no charm. She felt dirty just being in it. Olivia decided she would change into her comfortable pajamas when she got back to the room. Suddenly, something dark flashed in the corner of her eyes. Her gaze followed it.

When she saw the huge rat—its tail pink and long, its coat wet and patchy—she felt like icy fingers were grabbing her spine. In the blink of an eye, it bolted over her foot. Olivia's eyes tore wide as a high-pitched scream exploded from her lungs.

The bathroom door swung open and Christian stormed in.

"Ra-rat!" Olivia screamed again, pressing her back against the cold porcelain toilet as she pointed frantically at the rat in the corner of the room. In the heat of the moment, she completely ignored the fact that her pants were still around her ankles. Quickly, Christian attempted to use his foot to shove the squeaking rat aside, but it was too fast. It skittered away from him, heading right toward her again.

Standing and screaming again, she threw herself against the other side of the wall, pants still around her ankles. Like something possessed, the rat followed her as Christian scurried after it. With a loud squeak, it jumped between her legs, its bumpy tail touching her skin, and disappeared through a crack in the wall.

With a last scream escaping her lungs, Olivia jumped into Christian's arms. He stumbled backwards through the open bathroom door, and before they knew it, both of them lay on the red rug in the hallway—Olivia on top of him, still naked from the waist down.

"I felt it on me!" Her pants were hanging down one ankle now and her legs spread around his hips. Her head was turned, eyes fixed through the bathroom doorway, when she slowly pushed into a sitting position. It took a few seconds for her mind to switch from the rat horror to her current situation. She glanced down at Christian, who was silently buried underneath her, face up and staring. His hands were warm against her naked hips. The cold shiver that was running down her spine moments ago was replaced with something hot and tin-gling—she was on fire!

"What happened?" Mihai's voice shouted down the hallway. Olivia glanced up to see the keeper thunder toward them. Without a second to waste, she jumped up and fled into her bedroom, her pants dragging behind her, still attached to one ankle.

"Crazy Americans!" was the last thing she heard Mihai growl be-fore she slammed the door behind her. For a moment she listened if Christian was following her, but much to her relief, he didn't. With burning cheeks, she threw her head back against the wooden door, staring at the dark celling. *Oh my God! This must be is the most embar-rassing moment of my entire life! I hope he won't ever talk about this . . . not tomorrow, not in a thousand years! Please God, make him forget, forget, forget!*

CHAPTER ELEVEN

The castle looked different by morning. The sky was still cloudy, but a small splash of blue made it appear somewhat friendlier. The trees were no longer shrouded in fog, and the greens and reds and yellows of flowers were scattered around.

Christian yawned and stepped away from the window, rubbing the back of his neck as a soft groan escaped his lips. He looked at the bed he'd slept in and the groan deepened. He hadn't slept much last night. His thoughts had been filled with *her*.

"Olivia," he said under his breath, shaking his head.

He could still feel her body on his. His hands touching the softness of her hips. Her eyes, deep and penetrating. He gritted his teeth and rubbed the back of his head again. He'd have breakfast with her soon and would see those pretty eyes again; he looked forward to it and yet . . .

He walked out of the room. The castle was brightened by the light of day coming in through its small, iron-barred windows. It was a stark contrast to the night's flickering torches and dancing shadows. When he entered the kitchen, Olivia was already sitting at the small table, set up with cheese sandwiches from the fridge and fresh coffee she had just brewed for the two of them.

She gave him a warm smile as he sat down. "Good morning," she said like nothing had happened the previous night, like everything was totally and absolutely normal. It was like he was back to being her tour guide again.

Isn't that what you are? he asked himself as he chewed on the sandwich.

The keeper appeared suddenly, which seemed to be the only way he appeared anywhere. He was wearing the same woolen outfit that looked like period clothing, including the brown cloak with hood.

"Elena called," he growled in his usual fashion, pulling his hood back.

"Called?" Christian wondered. "Your phone has reception up here?"

"Landline." Was all he said before he let out a grunt and left without another word.

Christian and Olivia curiously watched him disappear. "Emm . . . and the message?" Christian hollered after him, half-irritated and half-amused. "Would be nice to know why she called . . ."

"I wonder why he didn't tell us there was a landline," Olivia said. "Didn't you need a phone last night? To call your mother?"

He frowned and looked at her. "Yeah, he could have. But I was able to get a text through to my mom. I had to stretch the phone out the hallway window."

"I mean you literally asked if there was internet so you could email your mother because your phone didn't work." She pushed her food around with her fork.

Christian nodded. "You'd think that would kinda be a no-brainer, but maybe he just needs a few years to warm up to us."

She smiled then tilted her head. "I wonder what the message was."

Christian looked up. "I'll ask him as soon as I'm done with break-fast."

"You can ask him now," Olivia whispered and raised her gaze. Christian turned around.

As if he'd been eavesdropping, Mihai was standing right behind Christian again, startling him.

"Jesus Christ," Christian said as his hand shot up to his chest. "Kinda hard to get used to that. Where did you even go?" Mihai narrowed his eyes in return.

"Why didn't you tell us about the landline?" Christian asked him. The old man's face was blank as his bearlike voice growled, "You didn't ask."

Christian threw Olivia a quick eyeroll before looking back at the keeper.

"Did Elena have a message for us when she called on the landline? The one I really needed last night?" He stressed the word *landline*, and the keeper grunted.

"She did," he answered.

Christian exchanged looks with Olivia again as they waited for a follow up. None came. Mihai looked unperturbed by their glances and seemed to be enjoying himself.

"Emm…" Christian said. "Would you mind telling us what the message was?"

"Of course not, just have to ask." He went ahead. "Elena said she feels too sick to meet you here today. She will come up tomorrow morning."

Christian saw Olivia's gaze lower and her lips bend in a frown. Before he could say anything else, the keeper continued, this time fixing his gaze on Olivia. "She wants me to take the American miss on a hike to show her the Rusu property."

Christian's eyes narrowed in suspicion. "On a hike in the Magura Forest?"

Mihai threw him a curt nod. "I know these woods well."

Is it just me, Christian wondered, *or is this whole thing getting weirder by the day?* He turned to Olivia and raised an eyebrow. Olivia gave a hesitant smiled. "That's nice of Elena. A little hike would be fun."

The keeper grinned, stretching his wrinkled face and exposing his yellow teeth.

Christian faked a smile. "Do you mind if I join?" he asked, curiously watching the keeper's grin vanish.

"Not at all," Olivia said, her smile turning genuine.

Mihai stepped forward, shaking his head slowly, almost disapprovingly. "Don't you have to go and check on your mother?"

"I'll just call from the newly discovered landline. She'll be fine." He kept his gaze on Mihai, who stared back before letting out a short grunt and walking off.

"Meet me in front of the gate at two," he instructed as he left, his cloak flapping with every step of his long legs.

I hope she doesn't think I'm creepy, Christian thought. He remembered the previous night, when he'd opened his eyes and saw her standing above him. It had felt like a dream; he'd almost reached out and pulled her into his arms. *Thank God I didn't.* He sighed with relief, bringing his cup of coffee to his lips. He stole a glance at Olivia. She smiled as she ate. She looked so innocent. The way her lips moved as she chewed, and how she occasionally tucked a loose strand of her soft hair behind her ear. *She's really pretty.*

He was glad he hadn't left her alone with Mihai. But why didn't he? Why did he care so much? Sure, the whole thing was weird, but it's not like she was in real danger. So, "Why?" The word slipped out of his mouth and he stiffened. Olivia looked up. She caught his gaze and stopped chewing.

"Did you say something?"

It was his turn to look away, letting his gaze fall on his steaming coffee cup.

"Sorry. Nothing important. Was just thinking out loud. Do you want to explore the castle some more before the hike? We still have to investigate the spooky attic."

She grinned. "I can live with that . . . if we skip the haunted dungeon today."

***

The gravel and dried yellow and orange fall leaves crunched under their feet as they walked through the walled-in courtyard of the castle. The air was thin and a bit cold, the sky still grey and grim. Olivia wore a black wool coat over blue pants and a pair of hiking boots she'd luckily brought from home. A crow was cawing from somewhere in the leafless sea of trees rising over the grey stone walls. Christian stopped next to her, rolling up the sleeves of his white shirt.

"You're not cold?" she asked.

"Yeah, I get hot quickly when I hike. Besides, this isn't Siberia," he replied and shoved her playfully with his shoulder. She giggled.

They reached the rusty iron gate and Christian looked around. "He told us to meet him here at two, didn't he?"

Olivia opened her mouth, but out of nowhere—as always—Mihai approached them from behind, dressed in a dark wool outfit, a rifle in his left hand. Olivia stared at the gun as Christian rolled his eyes in annoyance.

Mihai patted the rifle. "It is for our safety . . . against the bears."

Remembering the words of the couple the night the van had broken down, they both nodded, although Olivia more enthusiastically than Christian.

Mihai rested the rifle against his shoulder. "This way," he said and led them through a small wooden door in the wall and onto a trail.

Despite the gloomy feel, the woods and mountains were quite pretty. The fog had returned, but not as thick as before, and now, somehow, it gave the place a nice dramatic effect. The air around the woods smelled of fresh dirt and leaves.

Mihai was leading the way, and Olivia walked beside Christian, her arm occasionally brushing up against his. Olivia couldn't help but smile as she surveyed the peaceful forest, even stretching out a hand to touch the stiff branches of the trees.

"Someone seems to be enjoying this," Christian said in a hushed tone.

"I admit it was a bit creepy last night, but now it's almost like being in a Tim Burton movie. I love it!"

After about two hours, they came upon a large, round clearing filled with small stone houses whose walls and roofs looked crumbled and old. Most of the houses had fallen apart and were overridden by high grasses. A brown rabbit hopped past one of them.

"Looks like an abandoned village," Christian said.

"Whoever lived here was really well hidden," Olivia said.

Mihai led them though high, wet grass to an old well at the center of the abandoned village. It was made of round, grey rocks and was maybe six feet wide. It was surrounded by a patch of grass, most of which had grown as high as the well itself.

Using his rifle to split the grass, Mihai stepped next to the well. He took a short peek inside and then looked at the two. "Not many know this, but this well," he said, placing his gigantic hand on the stone edge, "is the real Well of Death. The other wells are just fakes."

"Well of Death?" Olivia asked and turned to Christian, who took a step toward the well to have a closer look.

"There is an old story about a well called the Well of Death," he explained, looking down the stretching darkness. Olivia joined him, leaning over the edge. It looked endless. Olivia could feel the cold rocks pressing against her legs.

"The story goes that a long time ago, there was a group of Turkish war prisoners who were ordered to dig a well. They were promised their freedom in return." He placed a hand on its wet rock wall. "They dug night and day, eager to be freed and return home to their families. But after they finished, they were all thrown inside."

Olivia gasped. "That's horrible!"

"Yeah," he agreed. "It's rumored that some of them survived the fall. You could hear their cries from the bottom of the well for months, living off the water from the well and insects. Until the winter came." His words were slow and intense. He shook his head and stared down the well. The foggy air around them had grown still. No rustling grass, no chirruping insects disturbed the woods.

"People believe that even now you can hear their cries if you look down the well and listen closely."

"Really?" Olivia whispered and placed both hands on the well, staring down into it.

They became quiet, watching the dark depths and picturing the agony of being trapped down there. The more they stared, the more the silence seemed to crack. Suddenly, a rustling noise coming from the woods startled them and they each let out a gasp. They jerked around to see a deer coming to an abrupt halt in the grass and turn on the spot the moment it saw them. Chuckling nervously, and with relief, they leaned against the well. Suddenly Christian pushed himself off, his eyes darting left and right.

"He's gone!" he said.

Olivia turned around and saw that Mihai was no longer with them. "Where'd he go?" she asked, circling the well as if she might find the man squatting behind it.

"Mihai!" Olivia called out for him, but Christian rushed over and grabbed her by her arm.

"Not a good idea. The woods are filled with bears. They are aggressive right now to protect their cubs," he warned.

In silence, they marched the grounds of the old village, but Mihai was gone. Christian kicked up a pile of dirt and grass.

"Where the hell did he go? He knows the woods can be a dangerous place without that rifle to scare the bears off."

The woods seemed even more silent now. The trees seemed to bunch together, drawing in closer around the village, almost as if they sensed the absence of Mihai—the armed person who knew the way back.

Olivia looked up. The clouds were getting thicker, darker. "Should we wait here for him? Maybe he'll coming back for us."

Christian shook his head. "We can't stay here, it's not safe. We have to find our way back."

She peered around and frowned when she saw the fog settling in. Christian noticed it too, cursed under his breath. Then he led the way back down the path of parted grass and out of the opening and back into the woods.

"The damn trees all look the same," Olivia said as they took a path that looked somewhat like the one they'd come from. "I didn't even notice how many paths there were when we first came out here."

"They are not human paths but animal trails." His voice softened. "But don't worry. We'll find our way back . . . someday."

She looked up at him with a faint smile.

He smiled. "Besides, if a bear shows up, I could easily distract it with my succulent flesh while you run away." He rubbed his arms, and Olivia covered her mouth to stop herself from laughing out loud.

"I'm pretty sure you won't taste all that good."

He gasped and pointed at himself. "You kidding? This is Romanian man-meat at its finest! You haven't tasted me, that's why you'd dare to say that."

She blushed and exhaled. Her fear had been replaced by something else. *You haven't tasted me.*

Christian slowed and came to a halt. The path they were on split into a fork. Standing in front of the two different options now, he looked around scratching his chin. Then he pointed to the one on the left, confidently. "That way."

They'd only walked for another minute or so when the strong, meaty smell hit Olivia's nostrils. It smelled like cat food, strong and fishy. She stopped and looked at Christian, who turned around with a puzzled look on his face.

"Do you smell that too?" she asked. He was about to say something when they heard the tiny wheezing.

"What was that?" Olivia asked with a panicked look on her face. The wheezing sound was followed by snapping branches—it sounded close.

Olivia saw a dark brown shadow move between the trees. She jumped next to Christian, a cold shiver running down her spine. Her hand slid around his arm and she squeezed tight. "I think I see a bear," she said, pointing. Christian's narrowed eyes froze on the same spot.

"Oh no," he muttered as his shoulders dropped. A few more sounds of moving branches and rustling leaves, and to their utter shock, a little bear cub rolled out of the brushes and onto the path. It spotted them, turning its head hesitantly as it blinked its small round eyes and twitched its nose. It took a few steps closer to them and purred, its tiny claws digging into fallen leaves and playing with something shiny—a can! Then a louder click was heard from the woods. Christian gently pushed Olivia backward, signaled her to slowly move away from the cub.

Olivia trembled and squeezed Christian's arm as they took slow steps backwards. "Maybe we can outrun it, it's just a cub," she whispered, her eyes moving into the woods where the last noise had come from. The cub purred and playfully hit the can as if it were a toy.

Christian touched her hand, carefully releasing it from his arm. He kept his eyes on the bear cub. "I want you to back up . . . slowly . . . until the cub is out of sight."

Olivia nodded, her heart racing.

Of course, Olivia you fool, its mother must be right around the corner!

***

Christian swallowed hard, steadying his nerves while the wheels in his head turned. *This is bad. Very, very bad!* If a bear cub was here now, then its mother wasn't far behind. As if that was all just games and play, which it probably was to the cub, it curiously followed their every step, hopping and kicking up leaves.

"Shoo! Get back!" Christian said in a hushed voice and shook his hands at the bear, but the harder they tried, the more interested it became. The bear cub let out its tiny growl, cutting the gap between them with each second.

Christian and Olivia started to back up faster and faster without running. Maybe the cub would turn around if it got too far away from its mother. Just as he was thinking it, a louder, angrier growl, ripped through the silent woods and shook the air around them. A moment later, a huge, dark brown bear emerged from the line of trees, snapping branches with its momentum and great bulk. Olivia shrieked as the huge bear leaped forward in front of the cub, only inches away from Olivia. It rose onto its two hind legs to swat at the air with its front paws. Throwing its head sideways, the bear opened its jaws, exposing its teeth in a terrifying growl. Without a second to waste, Christian leaped forward, placing himself between the bear and Olivia.

"Run!" he shouted, and the bear growled louder. Letting out a scared gasp, Olivia split to the side and ran.

I have to do something. I have to protect her!

***

The locket around her neck tapped against her chest as she ran, panting and praying. Olivia could hear Christian's voice echoing from behind her:

"Back! Ha! Shoo! Shoo!" Followed by the bear's angry growls.

How the hell could he possibly win a fight against a bear? Alone!

Olivia halted, her feet sliding against the dead leaves underfoot. He was sacrificing himself for her! She turned around and saw Christian on the ground, the massive bear towering over him.

"No!" she screamed and ran toward him. The bear raised its paw and was about to hit Christian, but it stopped the moment it heard Olivia's intense shouts.

"Hey, over here! Here! Look here!" she frantically called out to the bear. The animal's two massive paws hit the ground as its eyes focused on Olivia. It started toward her.

"What are you doing?!" Christian yelled and rolled across the ground onto his side.

"Making noise!" Olivia shouted back, watching helplessly as the bear started trotting toward her. Suddenly, she had an idea.

"That's it!" she said. "Making noise!"

With shaking hands, she fumbled for her phone. Smashing her fingers onto the screen, she searched for the air horn app she still had from an office Super Bowl party. A few hard taps onto the yellow trumpet icon, and the most annoying sound she had ever heard in her life thundered through the woods. Olivia hit the button again and again as low-quality trumpets and cheers blasted from her phone.

Amazingly, it worked. The bear stopped in its tracks as soon as the sounds blared, ears folded back as far as they could go, looking left and right in confusion over what was going on. Olivia stepped toward it and held out her phone as it played the long blasts over and over again.

The cub was the first to squeal in fear and flee into the woods. Its mother let out a last low growl, this time sounding more insecure than angry, then turned around to run after her cub. Olivia kept hitting that

air horn app, staring at the trees both bears had just disappeared behind, before she let her hand drop. She let out a long sigh of relief and
dropped onto her knees, a smile on her face.

Christian ran up to her and grabbed her hand to pull her up.

"Are you okay?" he asked, all panicky, still glancing around in case
Mama Bear came back for another go.

"I'm fine. I think." Her voice was shaky as she made it to her feet.
She took in a deep breath and let it out, chuckling, her hand still held
tight to his.

He shook his head, grimacing as he did.

"What's wrong? Are you hurt?" she asked.

He turned his right arm. "Just a scratch on my arm. It's nothing.
Really. We'll look at it later."

She nodded and exhaled again, tucking her phone back. "That was
crazy, huh?"

He didn't respond; he was focused on something on the ground.

"What is it?" Olivia asked.

Christian let go of her hand and walked over to the can the cub had
been playing with. He picked it up and sniffed it.

"Cat food," he said turning the can left and right as he read its
bright pink label with a white cat on it.

Olivia walked over and took the can out of his hands. "I thought I
smelled cat food. But why would there be cat food along the path?"

Christian narrowed his eyes. "That's a very good question."

"Do you think they stole the food from a farm or campsite?"

Christin tilted his head. "In Magura Forest? Possible, but not likely."

Olivia frowned and noticed Christian's eyes on her.

"What?" she asked, blushing. "You don't think I—"

"You saved me," he interrupted her. "I can't believe you did that for me."

"I can't believe that worked." She tapped her phone in her pocket. "Turns out that app has more use than damaging your eardrums."

He didn't smile, his eyes still set on her. "That bear could have killed me, but you . . . you saved me. Nobody but my mother would ever do such a thing for me. Does the world know how brave and self-less you are, Olivia Carter?"

Her smile waned. *The world only knows how boring I am,* she almost said but stopped just before the words could slip through her lips.

"It's nothing," she said. "Besides, you risked your life for me first."

His eyes softened and he laughed, the sound filled with his relief and gratitude. He grabbed the empty cat food can out of Olivia's hand and squeezed it into the upper front pocket of his white shirt. Then his gaze fell onto something in the distance.

"Hey, look!" he said and walked toward a dead tree, its rotten branches black and full of termite holes. "I recognize this tree." He stopped in front of it and looked around. Olivia strode over and stood beside him.

"Really?" she asked.

"Yes. I remember wondering what killed it when I spotted it on our way to the village. We're on the right path." He pointed at the path they'd been walking on right before the bear incident. "I was facing it downhill when we came, so going up the slope from here on should take us right back to the castle. Let's go."

Christian started walking carefully up the hill, glancing around behind him. Olivia followed closely, her hand snug around the phone in her pocket. Every small sound sounded like a growl, or a scratching paw, or a bear's heavy footstep. She walked faster.

He slowed down and when she caught up, he turned to her and looked at her closely. "Are you sure you're all right?"

She was able to hold his gaze this time. "Just shaken, but I'm okay."

Her eyes went to his upper arm, the slashes on his bloody clothes. "Are you okay though? That looks like it got you."

"I'm not dead, thanks to you. Now come, the castle is just up ahead."

***

It felt like that squeezing feeling around her chest stopped the moment she spotted the main gate and the grey stone castle finally came into view.

They found Mihai by the gate, walking up and down, looking nervous. When he saw them, his old face scrunched into a grimace of what could've been either relief or disappointment.

Before they could say anything, he placed his hands together as if in prayer, smiling wide like he was relieved to see them. "I feared the worst. I couldn't find you two and . . . and . . ."

"You couldn't find us?" Christian asked sternly. "Why don't we start with how you went missing in the first place?"

"We were by the well," Olivia chipped in. "But when we turned around you were gone."

Mihai shook his head. "No. No. I went to piss, you see. I told you that. You did not hear me, eh? I come back and you two were gone. I looked for you, but then I came back here to organize a search troop."

Olivia and Christian exchanged glances.

"So you went to the bathroom and then came back and we were gone?" she summarized his statement, a brow raised high.

Mihai shrugged his shoulders. "That's how it was. You shouldn't have left the village. I went for a piss. I don't piss in front of women."

Christian threw his hands up, his brows drawn in anger. "We looked for you! Where the hell did you go to piss? Russia?" He pointed at Olivia. "We were attacked by bears! She could have died!"

Mihai narrowed his eyes and spat on the ground. "Watch your tone, boy," he warned.

Christian clenched his fist and took another step toward Mihai.

"Christian! That's enough," Olivia cut in and held his arm, feeling his tense muscles. The two men were locked in an intense stare.

"Come on, we better go and take a look at your wound," she said, gently pulling at his arm. She could feel him relax.

Mihai shook his head. "I'm sorry if you got a scare in the woods. We better not hike again this season." Mihai's gaze wandered to Christian's shirt pocket, where the cat food can was sticking out. He stared for brief second before looking away. Did he know where it had come from? Maybe she was being paranoid.

"I better go," Mihai said. "I need to call off the search troop. Thanks to the Lord you are back safe. No need to make them come up here."

"Thank you," Olivia said, acting as normal as she could. Mihai nodded and walked a few steps toward the castle, but then turned once more.

"Before I forget," he said in his usual low, growling voice, "don't leave any food out. When I called down into the village, a farmer told me that bears had broken into his storage and stole a bunch of food. Even the cans."

Olivia and Christian exchanged puzzled looks.

"Yes, thank you, Mihai," Olivia said. Mihai threw her a curt nod, grunted, and left.

Olivia and Christian both watched him disappear inside the castle. Christian groaned. "I don't like this guy."

"I don't either," Olivia agreed. "But it might not be wise to pick a fight with the man who has the only gun in a lonely castle miles away from any other form of life. And it's getting dark again soon. If we left and your van broke down again . . . It's not like he actually tried to kill us. He just wasn't around to save us."

Christian sighed. "I still don't feel good about any of this."

"Me neither. Tomorrow I'll talk to Elena to see if a replacement for Mihai would be a good idea. Until then, we'll keep things low-key. Stay out of his way. Besides, what if he's telling the truth? We have no evidence that he's not. It would be very unjust to accuse him of . . . of what exactly?"

"Fair enough. But I hope you don't mind me sticking around until Elena shows up tomorrow. I won't leave until this whole situation has been looked at under a magnifying glass." Christian gave her a reassuring smile then shook his head.

"What?" Olivia wondered.

"Nothing. It's just . . . do you always try to see the best in people?"

She twisted her lips. "Unfortunately, yes."

Christian stepped closer, lifting a hand as if to caress her cheek. Her heart started pounding in anticipation of his warm touch. But then he pulled back. "There is nothing unfortunate about a kind heart, Olivia. It's the rotten people who abuse it that lose out in the end."

Olivia tugged at his arm. "Come on, let's go take a look at that wound."

"I might need some wine for the pain," Christian said.

"I think I can make that happen . . . if you come with me into the wine cellar. It's too dark and scary to go alone."

Christian nodded. "At least there won't be any bears down there."

They both laughed.

CHAPTER TWELVE

There's something I don't trust about that guy. Christian frowned each time he looked at the bandage around his arm. Luckily, it was only a few deep scratches that he could get stitched at the doctor's tomorrow. But how convenient that the only person with a rifle had slipped out to "use the bathroom" just as a couple of bears had been lured in with cat food. Christian had no real evidence, and yet, he had his suspicions nonetheless.

What terrified him even more were the what-ifs: What if Olivia had been alone with that man? What if she hadn't been able to think of that phone app? What if she'd gotten hurt, or worse?

He tried not to think of the worse, as it almost hurt in his chest. But why did he feel this way? He tried to tell himself that he was just a good tour guide. Olivia insisted on compensating him for his hours at the castle, but there was more to his worry than that of a "guide." These feeling were too intense to ignore and brush off.

"I don't like this guy. That gun would have been useful to scare off that bear," Christian said while they had dinner that night.

"My hands are still shaking!" Olivia said in an excited tone. She showed Christian the app with the blaring horn. "And I don't even watch football!" she added. "I only downloaded it for an office party because everybody else did, so I wanted to fit in."

"What made you even think of it?" he asked, genuinely impressed. She held his gaze without looking away as she recounted everything. As she did, he took in her childlike wonder, which spread through her eyes like fireworks.

"You have beautiful eyes," he said, and she stopped talking and blinked.

"What?"

"Uh . . . sorry. Nothing." Stop being creepy, he scolded himself. She's been through enough.

Toward the end of the dinner, she looked up at him. "Christian, I really appreciate your offer to stay . . . but if you have to go, it's fine, really. I will manage." She almost sounded convincing, until she added, "But if you really don't mind and don't need to be anywhere else, I would appreciate you staying another night."

"With what Mihai did today, I won't feel comfortable knowing there's no one else with you. So nope. Don't need to be anywhere else tonight." Liar. Mother and the girls need you. But this is more urgent. "I hope you don't take this the wrong way," he said. "But I think it's best if I sleep in your room tonight."

She lowered her eyes, so he added: "On the floor, of course. You don't have to worry about anything. I just don't like the idea of being down the hallway with such thick rock walls between us. Tomorrow . . ."

"I'm not worried about you sharing a room with me," she cut in. "I understand your concern. Things are getting a bit strange around here, but I also don't want to sound alarm over misunderstandings and shout false accusations. It's not easy for the Rusus, you know. Having someone else come in and take everything over, including a castle that has such significance for the Rusu family like this one. I don't want to be seem disrespectful. When I talk to Elena tomorrow, I will raise my concerns about Mihai and see what she thinks. Whoever of the Rusus has hired him must have done so for a reason."

He nodded. "Tomorrow, we'll figure things out. Talk to Elena and hopefully leave this castle and get you into a guest house in town. You know, one that's not watched by a creepy guy who leaves us to the bears."

Olivia frowned. "I think you're overreacting, Christian. It wasn't his fault that a bear attacked us. It's not like he called the bear to us. We just got unlucky."

"Maybe. Still, I don't think you need to stay here alone. At least let me hire more staff from town, get the cook back, maybe some maids?"

Olivia frowned. "Maids? Like I'm some old lady in waiting?"

"Don't want to help the local economy? Some folks in town have been without work and would be glad to have a job." He grinned. He knew he was using her own kindness against her.

"All right. If it helps the locals."

He smiled and stared straight at her, hoping the smile wouldn't come off as creepy. "I won't lay a hand on you. You can trust me."

"I trust you. You were willing to give your life for me today. You can stay in my room if it helps you feel all knight-like. Like the protector of a fair maiden that's not that fair."

Christian laughed. "Was that a dirty joke?"

"Was it?" She smiled.

***

The fire in the hearth crackled, casting a soft, dim light over the room. The air was silent, but thick. Each time their eyes met, they'd glance away. Olivia was also more than embarrassed by the cat pajamas she was wearing. The cute little black kittens printed on the white fleece pants and long-sleeved shirt had been her favorite PJs. Now they seemed ridiculous. Christian was making a bed near the fireplace, dressed like a normal person, still wearing his jeans and his white shirt that was shredded and stained with blood on his arm.

"Here, you'll need this," Olivia said and tossed a pillow at Christian from her bed. The pillow hit his face just as he looked up.

"Ouch, that hurt."

"No it didn't. It's just a pillow." She giggled and timidly pulled back a strand of her brown hair that had fallen over her face. He smiled and fluffed the pillow.

"It hurt mentally. I deserve some knightly respect after saving the lady today."

"If I remember correctly, I saved you. But in case you need more, there's plenty more where that came from. Just let me know." She gestured at the many pillows on the bed.

"If that's the case, I'd like another—" the second pillow hit him in the same spot on his head. Olivia laughed even harder.

"Okay, that one really hurt," he said with a smile, running a hand through his thick head of hair.

She reached for another pillow. "Her ladyship has another, if Sir Christian so desires."

"All right then, how about I give it a try?"

He grabbed one of the pillows she'd tossed at him and held it over his head, aiming at her. Olivia laughed and stretched out her hand to protect her face as she retreated to the far end of the bed.

"No don't," she pleaded, glancing at his arm that held the pillow aloft. His muscular bicep filled his shirt.

"Do what? Oh, you mean . . . this?" He tossed a pillow at her—softly. It barely touched her face, but she dramatically stumbled back, falling on the bed. She groaned and rubbed her face.

Christian gasped and rushed to her side. "Are you okay?"

She said nothing, her face still buried in a pile of pillows and blankets.

"I'm sorry, Olivia. I thought I barely threw it and—"

He stopped the moment her body began to shake with laughter. She rose from the pile of pillows. Christian rolled his eyes and gave her shoulder a soft punch.

"I take back my apology." He went back to making his bed on the floor with the extra blankets and pillows. "But what do I expect from someone in cat pajamas."

Olivia sat up, pushing the stubborn strands of her hair back. "Hey! Low blow!"

He looked up with a grin and dropped one of the pillows at the top of the blanket he'd spread out on the floor. "Excuse me, my lady. May I have my other pillow back?" he asked, smoothing out the blanket.

The pillow thumped against the side of his head, and Olivia giggled again.

"I'll be a gentleman and let that one slide."

"How noble of you," she said.

He glanced up, and she smiled before looking away. There was no way she could hold that gaze, not with how intense it was.

"I'll uh . . . get out of this if that's okay?" he asked, looking down on his pants and then pointed at the wooden room divider in the corner of the room next to the fireplace. She nodded without looking up.

He walked behind the room divider. Olivia waited until he was out of sight before staring at it. She noticed a small crack in the middle and looked away. Pressing against the headboard of the bed, she listening to the sound of his pants unbuckling. She heard him wince; he'd probably released the sleeve around his right arm.

Don't look! Don't look!

But as if something else was controlling her body, her face turned toward the divider once more—and she looked. A hot rush of excitement spread though her entire body when she saw Christian's muscular abdomen through the crack. He stood half-naked on the other side. God, he is all muscles! She jerked her head away, her hands shaking.

"Umm . . . So I'll just come out now, with boxers on," he said.

Good!

Olivia bit her lip at her thoughts. "Yeah, that's fine. I don't have pants for you but my workout t-shirt is hanging over the chair next to the divider. You could change your shirt if you want. It might be large enough."

"Thanks."

She saw him step out from behind the divider to grab the blue t-shirt from the chair. He was only wearing boxers and his entire naked chest was now revealed. The soft light of the fire glistened on his tan, muscular skin. Gosh, he had an amazing body! He looked up for a second as he grabbed the shirt and put it on. Olivia turned away quickly. She could feel her palms start to sweat. Had he seen her watching him? While Christian wasn't necessarily built like a body builder, he had a lean, naturally muscular frame.

Her eyes fell on the bandage on his upper arm. It was bloody. There was a dark red patch that spilled down his arm in light streaks.

She saw the scratches when she watched him clean his own wound and put the bandage on earlier in the library. Long and red, three of them about an inch deep and five inches long.

"You're bleeding again!" She hurried toward him.

"It's nothing. I'm fine." He held her gaze. "It was just a scratch."

"We'll need to get you stitched tomorrow." She grabbed his arm and pulled him to the bed. "Sit, I'll put a new bandage on," she said.

"Woah! Yes, ma'am." He chuckled and sat. "It's really just a scratch. I'm sure it'll heal by morning," he said as she walked around the bed to retrieve her bag. "What do you have there?" he asked as she approached.

"Just a little first aid kit I travel with." She placed the little red box on the bed and reached out for his arm. "Now hold still."

The wads of cotton she used, dipped in over-the-counter wound sanitizer, soon turned dark as she cleaned the scratches.

"You're quite good at this," he said, and she smiled.

"Better than you," she said, holding up the used cotton balls to show him the mud on them. She dipped a fresh wad into the sanitizer, feeling the coolness against her fingers, and dabbed the length of the wound, tracing it until it was a light pink. "So, are all your tours this . . . exciting?"

He scoffed. "Oh, it's not a real tour until someone gets attacked by a wild animal. But I don't think I've ever had this many wild adventures before. You seem to attract them."

She looked up sharply.

"It's a good thing."

Olivia smiled and placed the stained wad into a wrap. She used a Q-tip to gently put ointment on the cleaned scratches.

"You didn't even flinch one tiny bit. I'm impressed." She still had one hand on his wrist as she examined his arm.

He laughed. "Don't tell me American men would flinch like little boys over a tiny scratch like this."

She grinned and raised his arm to wrap a bandage around the pink and red flesh. "We have many brave men in America." She briefly frowned. "I just have yet to meet them."

"Are you saying that none of the men in your life would have saved you today?"

"Saved me from a bear?" She laughed out loud. "They couldn't even keep it in their pants for me." She shook her head in amusement, as if he had just made the most ridiculous joke. "My ex save me from a bear . . . too funny."

"Then they were a waste of time, anyway, if they couldn't see what was right in front of them."

She smiled sadly. "Not too much, according to them."

He frowned. "As I said, little boys not worth a woman's time."

The words floated around in her head as she turned away from him and put away the kit.

"You know what else I think?" Christian said and got to his feet. He was turning his arm, looking at the bandage in approval.

She faced him. "What?"

"I think you are one of the most amazing people I've ever met. Kind, brave, and selfless. A rare diamond."

Olivia laughed, but he looked so serious. They stared at each other for a moment, the air thickening around them. Her cheeks flushed as she looked away.

"Are you sure that will be comfortable enough?" She nodded at his improvised bed on the floor.

"It will."

She watched as he lay on the floor, carefully avoiding making too much contact with his injured arm. It looked uncomfortable, and it was going to be impossible to avoid rolling onto his arm all night.

"See? Perfect," he said, grinning at her.

She shook her head. "No."

"What?"

"You can't sleep on the floor with your wound. Take the bed instead."

He shook his head. "I can't let you sleep on the floor."

"Then we'll both sleep on the bed so nobody sleeps on the floor," she said.

He lay still as if expecting her to say she was kidding. But she didn't.

"All right then," Olivia mumbled and grabbed a pillow, making her way to the floor. "Then we'll both sleep on the floor."

"Okay, okay." He sighed as he stood up. "You are one stubborn lady."

She smiled. "Maybe. No one's ever told me that before."

He rose and stared at her. "Well . . . Here I am telling you now. You are one stubborn lady." He held her gaze a moment longer then tossed the pillow on the bed. "And stubborn is kinda cute," he added and stretched out on the bed. Olivia laid down on her side of the bed, her heart thumping fast.

They both lay at opposite edges, a considerable space in between them. Olivia turned the nightlamp on her nightstand off. Now, the only light in the bedroom came from the crackling fireplace. A clock ticked somewhere in the room.

It's funny how you focus on these tiny sounds when you can't sleep, Olivia thought: the crackling wood in the fireplace, clothes ruffling, tiny movements, deep breaths. She wondered what Christian was thinking. She could picture his perfect body next to her. So close.

She tapped her fingers together and nibbled her lip as she tried to think of something to say.

"Are you sleeping?" she asked. Her voice was soft in the quiet room. When he didn't respond, she felt a momentary disappointment. Then his voice cut in.

"No. Can't sleep."

She bit her lip again, feeling a fluttering in her stomach. She turned toward him. "Why can't you sleep?"

"Could you please not look at me? Please turn around again," he said, and she shivered, feeling those butterflies inside her stomach.

His words in her head spiraled out of control. Why didn't he want her to look at him? Was he attracted to her? Did he long for her the way she longed for his touch? Impossible! Just look at him! What would someone like him want with someone like me? Her sadness was numbing.

"I know you're worried I think you might make a move on me," she whispered and turned away. "Don't worry. I don't. I know I'm not the sort of woman that could—"

Before she could say anything else, she felt that ruffle of sheets and when she turned around, she saw he was right next to her. She held her breath, feeling the heat of his body next to hers. Her heart thumped out of control as a tingling sensation rushing through every inch of her body. She felt paralyzed.

He leaned forward, closing the remaining gap between them, and their lips touched. His lips were soft on hers.

"You kidding?" he said, pulling away for a moment. "You're all I've thought about since we met."

She could feel his breath between those whispers and shuddered, her body burning from desire. They kissed, their bodies rubbing against each other—the soft sounds of their lips, the muffled moans, and the gentle ruffling of clothes.

His hand found her face, gently stroked her cheek as he broke the kiss.

"Are you sure this is what you want?" he asked, looking into her eyes. She looked back into his and leaned closer.

"I don't think I've ever wanted anything this much," she replied with half-shut eyes. Her heart was drumming in her ears as the heat of her body burned her skin. There was no denying the flames she felt tearing through her body, and the longing swirling deep inside her. She craved him, more than anything else in her life, more than all that money, and that was all she knew.

She bit her lip, moving closer to him, inch by inch, until their lips touched again. That was all it took, the permission he had asked for.

The sheets ruffled as their hands moved to shuffle out of their clothing.

"Ouch!" Christian winced when her hand touched his upper arm.

"Sorry," she said.

He slid his hand to her lower back, pulling her closer. "It's fine," he whispered into her ear and gently nibbled on it, kissing and flicking the lobe with his tongue. She shuddered and pressed herself into him, her head low as he helped her slip out of her shirt and pull her pants down over her ankles.

They lay naked in bed, the warmth of their bodies pressed together. She'd never had anyone touch her with so much care and desire. The way he ran his tongue over her body was nothing she had ever experienced before.

"Christian," she moaned softly when his lips found her neck, setting her body on fire. She lay on her back and pulled him onto her. He looked into her eyes again, as if for one last confirmation, and she pressed her hands against his hip to pull him inside of her. She held her breath when she felt his hardness between her legs, sparking waves of sensation, which rolled through her body, making her shudder.

Soft groans and grunts escaped their lips as their bodies moved in unison, slowly grinding back and forth. Their pace intensified as her hands caressed his muscular back, feeling the heat and the sweat. And then she felt her body stiffen as something exploded deep inside her. Like fireworks, she thought as she closed her eyes. How did I get so lucky?

CHAPTER THIRTEEN

The best things in life happen when you least expect them. Christian's father had often spoken these words, and they rolled around in Christian's head as he slowly woke up. Olivia was snuggled up next to him. He felt the warmth of her body and smiled when he saw her head resting on his chest, her hand next to her face. She had a small smile on her lips. He wondered what she was dreaming about.

He leaned over and kissed her on her head. She blinked slowly and opened her eyes.

"Lucky bastard," he said.

"What?" she asked, tilting her head to look at him, her eyes now fully open and fixed on him.

"Me." He kissed her on her lips, more demanding this time. Then he playfully nibbled on her lower lip. Her giggles filled the room.

"Don't eat me, please."

"But I want to."

He smirked, and she hit his shoulder.

He stared at her as she rested her head on him, her soft curls tickling his bare chest. The warmth of her breath touched his skin, and her beautiful brown eyes looked deep into his.

"If you keep staring at me that way, I won't be able to let you leave this bed," he said and gently stroked her chin. *Her skin is so soft,* he thought as he squeezed her against himself. Everything felt perfect. He felt like he could hold her like this forever. *Is this what they call love?*

"I could never have dreamt of meeting someone like you," he said, and she lifted her gaze, still with her beautiful smile.

"After all we've been through . . . hope you mean that in a good way?" she added, and he chuckled.

"Definitely. It feels like we've known each other forever, even though we've just met. Is that weird?" he asked.

"I have never felt like this before, but I don't think it's weird at all. Not even close. That bear attack was crazy. We are not."

"That bear was crazy," he said and they both laughed. "I would have made for a disappointing dinner."

"I doubt that." Olivia raised her head and looked at him. "You're pretty sweet."

"Not as sweet as you are." He pulled her in for another kiss. "But just so you know, I'll have to charge extra for last night. That part of the tour was an add-on."

"So you do this add-on a lot then?"

He knew she was joking, but she also had a look in her eyes, like there was a part of her that was serious. He couldn't help but laugh.

"I'm taking care of five women. There's not much time for add-ons like this. And even if there was, it's not me. I need to connect with a woman to be intimate, and so far, that hasn't happened that often. Never like this, that's for sure."

Her fingers gently stroked his arm and he held her close for a moment longer.

"How about breakfast?" He kissed her forehead, then pushed his feet off the bed. The rug felt cold after the warmth of the blankets.

She nodded and made to get up. "Sounds good."

"You going somewhere?" Christian asked and watched as she shifted to the other side of the bed.

"Breakfast?" she said.

"I'm making you breakfast, so just relax and I'll be right back."

She snuggled under the sheets and grinned. "Yes, sir."

"I won't be long, my lady." He leaned over and sealed her lips with his. When he pulled away, she gazed up at him, her cheeks flushed. "I could get used to that look," he whispered and let the back of his hand graze her cheek. "Now will you excuse me? Her ladyship expects breakfast."

***

Christian had a skip to his step as he walked out of the room and into the dim hallway. Judging by the light coming thought the small windows, it must have been late morning. *Walking on air*, he though. *So this is how it feels?*

He almost whistled as he stepped down the enormous stairs, past the old paintings and metal knights. The cheerful feeling disappeared, however, as soon as he heard the voices in the great hall.

"Oh, there he is now!" he heard the angry voice as the great hall came into view. He saw Elena and Alina, and they didn't look pleased. Alina was sitting on one of the sofas next to the fireplace while Elena marched toward Christian. She looked ready to explode, her face purple. He braced himself for the coming storm.

"Mihai told me you slept in her room last night! I should have known better than to trust a man, not even the town's so-called angel!" she shouted in his face. "I paid you to show that helpless girl Romania, not what's in your pants!"

Her voice echoed through the hall, bouncing off the walls. Christian opened his mouth to speak but was cut off by Elena's rants.

"I should have known; you men are all the same!" she kept glancing at Alina as if expecting backup. "I trusted you," she continued, her face contorted in disgust, as if she smelled something foul. "What did you tell her, huh? That she is special? That you have never felt like this before?"

Once again, Christian opened his mouth to speak but she cut him short. "I will tell you this, while you were here on some romantic getaway"—she fell silent, waiting for the echoes of her voice to die down—"your mother has gotten worse. She is in the hospital as I speak."

"Hospital?" Christian said. "What? Since when?"

"You would know that already if you weren't so busy chasing after an American heiress," Elena answered.

He looked up when he heard Olivia's voice from the stairway. "What's going on? I heard voices and—" Her words cut off when she saw the horrified look on Christian's face. He glanced away.

Elena, still with an unpleasant look on her face, walked up to Olivia and grabbed her hand. "His mother is unwell."

"How terrible. I'm so sorry!" Olivia said. She walked over to Christian. "You should go to her now. They need you."

He looked at her and then at Elena.

"Don't worry," Olivia said. "I'll be fine with them here. Your family needs you now."

He nodded and realized his hands were shaking. The last thing he wanted to do was picture his mother dying in a hospital bed. He wanted to ask Elena how bad it was, what state his mother was in, but at the same time, her answer terrified him.

"I'll call you on the landline as soon as I can," he said to Olivia.

She rubbed his arm, mouthing the words, *go now.*

He nodded and looked at her one last time, then turned to rush out the door.

***

The van revved noisily as he tore through the driveway and hurried down the road, dust rising behind him and fading with the castle. The weight of the news of his mother and the thought of leaving Olivia behind were mixing into a distasteful mess in his head—and heart.

CHAPTER FOURTEEN

O livia recounted the story of the bear attack over breakfast in the dining hall. It felt good telling someone about the encounter and how brave Christian had been. Alina looked horrified, letting out dramatic gasps and clasping a hand over her mouth each time.

"That sounds terrifying," Elena said.

"It was," Olivia agreed. She told them about the app on her phone that had scared the bear off. "The bear cub was cute, but its mother . . . I felt the ground shake when she attacked."

Alina shook her head in shock.

Olivia chuckled, then sighed, her mind straying to Christian and that horrified look on his face before he left. She wondered where he was now and how his mother was doing.

Elena and Alina exchanged looks, and Alina stood up from her chair. "I'll be right back. I have to go to the bathroom," she said.

"Do you need me to show you where it is?" Olivia asked.

Alina looked at her mother before responding. "I'll be fine. I've been here with Uncle Andrei before."

Olivia nodded, a little embarrassed. "Yes, of course. It's your family's castle after all."

After Alina left, Elena talked about taking Olivia on a trip to the neighboring village.

"I feel much better today, and I'd love to take you. It has a beautiful town center. I think a day trip over there would do you some good. There will be no bears, I promise." She grinned and Olivia smiled. The last time she'd tried leaving the castle, she'd ended up in the middle of an abandoned, creepy village, fending off an angry bear. A trip to a real village—with people and away from the woods—would be nice.

"That sounds wonderful," Olivia said, lifting a glass of water to her lips. "I wouldn't mind getting out of this castle. Don't get me wrong, it's beautiful, but it's so far away from people and—"

"And let me guess," Elena said, leaning toward her. "Mihai?"

Olivia lowered her gaze to her plate. Her eggs and bread were untouched.

Elena let out a loud laugh. "Don't feel bad. You are not the first person intimidated by him."

Olivia looked up at her, feeling suddenly relieved. "No?"

"Of course not! I mean look at him. Those weird clothes and the way he grunts and growls. I'm always telling him to stop sounding like an animal; it scares people."

Olivia smiled. "I'm sorry for even bringing it up."

"Oh, please don't. I'm glad you did so I can put your nerves at ease. I have known Mihai since childhood. He is as trustworthy as he is scary looking. You will get used to his ways. But he's good to have around. People have already started talking about Andrei's American heiress. You don't want unwelcome visitors up here. Mihai will keep you safe."

Olivia frowned. "I'm sorry for doubting him."

"Please don't. It's not like he's as handsome as Christian," Elena said and let out a cackle. Olivia blushed.

A few minutes of silence followed while they ate, then Olivia remembered something. "Could we wait for Christian's call before we go to the village. I want to know how his mother is doing and if he needs anything."

"Of course, my dear. We can all wait together."

"Thanks."

"He is a wonderful man, isn't he?" Elena said.

"Christian?" Olivia felt her insides stir at the thought of the night before. She managed a smile and a nod. "Yes, he's . . . incredible."

***

Alina peeked over her shoulder several times before turning around a corner, down the hall, and up the stairs. She mistakenly opened the doors to several other rooms until she finally found Olivia's room and entered it. She knew her mother would keep Olivia at that table until she found what she came for.

That is the thing about mother, she thought as she admired the room—the lavish bed and drapes—*she talks too much.*

"Such a big place." Alina let her fingers run over the furniture on her way over to the bed. Her eyes strayed to the fireplace, and she smiled with longing.

The bed looked soft, and she was tempted to lay in it and pretend that this was her life, that this was how she woke up every day: wrapped in silk and soft linen, a warm breakfast waiting for her.

She's so lucky, she thought without a hint of spite. Although she liked Olivia, she couldn't help but feel jealous of someone who had so much. She pushed the thought away and focused on the task at hand.

She looked around for Olivia's belongings. She found her bag and lifted it onto the bed, pausing to listen for any sound. The hall outside was quiet, so she continued, carefully unzipping the bag and going through the items. What she was looking for wasn't there. Her eyes wandered the room and found the cellphone on the nightstand. She walked over and held it up, rubbing the black plastic casing with her thumb. She took the phone and was about to slip it into her small purse when her eyes fell on something shiny on the nightstand next to the lamp. She paused and narrowed her eyes. It was some kind of necklace with a locket attached to it. She picked it up and placed the locket on her palm and stroked the edges. She'd seen it before. She closed her eyes and tried to remember. "Yes!" She opened her eyes again and snapped her fingers. Olivia had shown it to Elena, talking about a picture of her parents inside it.

She pushed on the small button and the locket clicked and opened. She stared at the picture of that happy family for a long time before closing the locket again. *I'll take this instead,* she thought to herself and placed the phone on the nightstand where the locket was.

With one last glance around the room, to make certain everything was the way she'd found it, she slipped out quietly. Oddly enough, she felt a mix of emotions: pride at accomplishing her mother's task, but also guilt over what she'd done.

***

"I'll take a shower," Olivia said, pushing her chair back. "The water will do me some good. I won't be long," she said just as Alina walked in. Alina seemed a little out of breath, her face flushed. She probably got lost in the endless hallways that all look alike.

"Are you all right, Alina?" Olivia asked.

"She's fine," Elena answered. "Sometimes the food she eats doesn't agree with her. Her stomach has always been sensitive, isn't that so?"

Alina nodded and rubbed her forehead as she took a seat next to her mother.

"I'm sure I have some pills to help your stomach," Olivia said. "Do you want to come with me?"

"How kind. Alina, go with her."

Alina rose from her chair again. "Yes. Thanks."

***

Followed by Alina, Olivia entered her bedroom and drew in a sharp breath. *It still smells like him,* she thought with a smile. Walking over to her bag, she pictured his pretty face and the feel of his lips on hers. But, once again, worry gripped her as she wondered what he was doing now and how his mother was.

It'll be fine, she tried to tell herself while she riffled through her pack in search of her pills. She frowned when she felt nothing. She went through her bag once more. It took a few moments, but she found the pills at the bottom of the bag, wrapped inside one of her shirts.

"Weird." She stared at the bottle. She always kept her pills in the left corner pocket of her bag to make them easier to find; but then again, last night had been unusual. She walked over to hand Alina the pills.

"I'll hop in the shower real quick. You can wait here if you want," Olivia said and gathered her things. Shampoo, towel, fresh clothes, and her necklace to put on after the shower, which she thought was on the nightstand. Maybe in the covers of the bed.

Olivia lifted every pillow—twice—and shook the sheets three times each.

"What are you looking for?" Alina asked.

"My necklace."

"The one you showed my mother?" Alina asked. Olivia nodded.

Together they searched around for it, frantically looking through each piece of clothing, furniture, even under the bed. Minutes passed and still nothing. Olivia began to panic as she paced in front of the bed, then stopped to think.

"Where did I put it?"

She searched the drawers once more—nothing. The bed creaked when she climbed on it and pushed aside the blankets and pillows again, running her hand down the edge of the mattress and bedframe to see if it had somehow fallen in. The pillows fell off to the floor when she crouched down to check under the bed for the third time.

Still nothing.

"What is it, dear?" Elena's voice came from behind her. Olivia turned around, breathing heavily.

"She can't find it," Alina explained with a frown.

"Find what?"

"It's missing. My . . . my necklace." Olivia's voice shook as she touched the bare space on her neck. "I can't . . ." Her words were broken by an exasperated gasp as she tossed a pillow and once again went through her bag. "I can't find it."

"Can you describe it to me?" Elena asked. Alina remained silent as Elena drew closer and joined in the search.

"It's the silver locket I showed you. It's the only thing of my mother I have left. I always have it with me. I don't"—she sighed and lowered her voice—"I don't go anywhere without it."

"Then it must be here. Come, we'll find it," Elena offered, and even though Olivia politely expressed her skepticism, they still continued.

After a while Elena looked up, arching her back and rubbing her waist. Olivia noticed.

"You should sit down," Olivia suggested. "I can manage."

"I'm fine. Now, let's retrace your steps. When was the last time you saw it?"

"Yesterday. I thought I put it on this nightstand," Olivia said, her mind rewinding from that magical night all the way to the morning hike. When she thought more about the hike, she gasped and glanced at the two women.

"The bear attack! What if . . ." She lowered her voice, nibbling on her lower lip as she thought. "Could I have somehow dropped it in the woods during the attack?"

"It seems logical." Elena walked over to Olivia. "You know how terrified you were; it's very easy to miss these things."

"Not that necklace." She sighed and went back to the nightstand by the bed.

"I thought I had it on last night, when I took it off and placed it here," she touched the nightstand. "Or . . ." She paused. Or could it have been elsewhere? She was sure she'd had it on last night. But it made more sense to have lost it during the attack.

Disheartened, Olivia reached for the bed and sat down. "I have to go back and look for it. If it's not here then it must be out there." She felt racked with guilt, like she had abandoned her mother while she had the night of her life. *This is supposed to be our journey, and I left you behind.*

"That's a good idea," Elena said. "I will send Mihai to go with you. And Alina as well. Three pairs of eyes are better than two."

Alina lowered her eyes, grumbling. "I don't want to go out there."

Elena's eyes snapped to her daughter. "What was that?"

"I . . ." Alina tried saying but swallowed the words without completing them.

"Fine!" Elena sighed. "I will go help look for it."

"That's not necessary, Elena," Olivia said. "It's fine, really. Mihai and I will go while you wait here."

"No, my dear, I'll go with you," Elena insisted, her voice softening. "It's the least I can do. After all, I was the one who arranged for you to stay in this castle. And the doctor said exercise will do me good."

There was no point trying to argue with Elena, and a third party seemed like a good idea. Olivia glanced at Alina, who was still staring at the floor, her brows drawn together tightly, her eyes filled with fear. *Was she that terrified of the woods?*

"Thank you so much for your help." Olivia smiled. "We should head out soon. I can shower later."

***

Elena watched Mihai and Olivia through the small hallway window. They were waiting outside for her in the courtyard.

The necklace shimmered as it slid from Alina's soft hands into Elena's wrinkled palm. Alina's face was full of worry. She hesitated before letting go of the necklace.

Elena's grin morphed into a scornful look when she saw the expression on her daughter's face.

"Stop it, Alina."

"But—"

"But nothing!" She clasped her hand, covering the necklace. "I've told you I'm not going to hurt her. Just a little scare, that's all."

Alina's lips shook.

"Oh, now what?" Elena asked. Alina sniffled, then sobbed, and then she was full-out crying.

"Get a hold of yourself!" Elena jerked her gaze back to the window, panic on her face, but when she saw that neither Mihai nor Olivia had heard the sounds of her daughter's blubbering, she grabbed Alina by her arm and dragged her down the hall.

"Like so often, I wonder if I was the one who suckled you. Stop crying! You're ruining everything," she snapped at Alina, throwing her hand high into the air. But Alina wouldn't stop sobbing; she jerked herself free from Elena's grip and ran off with her face buried in her hands.

"Stupid girl," Elena mumbled to herself when Mihai suddenly appeared down the hallway.

"We are just going to scare the American girl, is that true?" he asked, his fat fingers clasped together. He growled and his eyes narrowed.

Elena scoffed and shook her head. Then she took a deep breath. "We'll go on with the plan just as we discussed, but my simple daughter doesn't need to know that. This American has no family left. With her gone and no other heirs named, I will have a strong case fighting in court for what's rightfully mine!"

Mihai nodded. "As long as I get my money," he growled.

"You will…more than you can spend."

The front doors opened, and Olivia stepped inside the castle, straightening her jacket. She managed a smile. "There you are. All ready to go?"

Elena mustered a smile. "Ready as can be."

CHAPTER FIFTEEN

The van bounced around a curve. Christian's arm glistened with sweat, his hand tight against the wheel as he steadied the vehicle, his other hand holding his phone.

"Come on, come on!" he pleaded to the phone. Zero bars still.

Dust clouds rose on either side of the van as the tires tore over the small road. The woods soon disappeared behind him, slowly easing into the vast openness of the farmhouses and fields at the foot of Magura Mountain. The colors of nature sprang up all around him, pushing back the greyness of the forest.

Thoughts filled with guilt racked his mind as his foot pressed the gas pedal all the way to the floor. *Where were you when they needed you? They must have tried calling,* he kept thinking as he gripped the wheel tighter.

Suddenly, just as he passed the first house in the village, his phone beeped.

"Thank God! Finally!" He sighed with relief as his fingers frantically brought up the keypad. He dialed his mother.

"Connect already!' he shouted. The phone rang for what felt like forever.

The phone clicked and he heard his mother's voice.

"Hello? Hello?" he said. He'd been expecting frantic words and wails, or worse.

"Christian? Is that you? Are you all right?" she said.

"Am I all right?" he asked. "What's going on with you? Are you at the hospital?"

"At the hospital? Why would I be at the hospital?" his mother said. "You're starting to worry me. Is something the matter?" She paused. "Did your stay with the American woman at that dreadful castle not go well? I texted you the place is cursed."

Christian didn't understand what was going on. He exhaled and slowed down the van. "No. I'm fine and the tour is going"—he scratched his chin—"very well. But I thought you were ill, so I left early."

"Ill? No. I was a bit weak yesterday but nothing too serious. Everyone here is fine. The girls are asking if you are now a prince and will marry a princess."

Why would Elena say that Mom was ill?

"Christian?" his mother said.

Why would she lie about her health? Make me storm out of this place?

The realization hit him like a hammer on the head.

"To get rid of me!" he shouted as he slammed hard on the brakes.

"What? What are you talking about?" His mother sounded worried.

"Mom, listen. I gotta go!"

"Go? Back to Magura Castle? Christian! What's going on?"

Taking a quick look around him, he saw the road was practically devoid of traffic except for a man on a cart being pulled by a grey donkey. Christian turned the van around.

"Hopefully nothing. I'll call you later." He ended the call before she could say anything. He quickly changed gears and urged the car back up the road. All he could think of was Olivia. He tried to keep the bad thoughts at bay—it was a long drive back up to the castle—but his heart betrayed him, thumping so hard against his chest it almost hurt.

What are you up to, Elena?

***

Olivia set off with Mihai and Elena. The woods were as silent as usual, the fog thick, and the leaves on the ground just as dry as they'd been the day before. Birds screeched in the sky, which was blocked by the thick, dark branches of the trees stretching high above.

They'd been walking for a while when Elena suddenly gasped and held her chest.

"Are you all right?" Olivia asked and went over to her.

"I . . ." Elena sighed and shook her head. "I think I just need to take a little rest here, on this rock. My old bones don't keep up as well as I thought they would."

Mihai stepped forward and looked at Olivia. "The place where the bear attacked should be just around the corner. Is that right, Olivia?"

She nodded. "Yes, I think so." She pointed down the path. "It was right after that dead tree over there."

"Good." He turned to Elena. "Just rest here and scream if you see a bear." He tapped his hand against the rifle resting against his shoulder. "I'll scare it off. Just try to run my way."

"Yes," Elena panted, out of breath. "I . . . will . . . scream for you . . . then run your way." She huffed and fanned herself as she leaned against the large rock. Olivia felt terrible. She shouldn't be the one left alone. If a bear turned up, she couldn't even run—unlike Olivia who was young and healthy. Not that it was the best strategy, but still.

Olivia shook her head. "It would be better if Mihai stays here with you, Elena. It's just around the corner, as you said. I can do a quick run and be right back.

"Are you sure?" Elena sounded concerned.

"Yes. I also have my phone on me. The horn app worked before. It'll work again."

"Good. Hurry then so I don't have to worry about you too much," Elena said.

Olivia turned and walked alone down the foggy path.

It's nothing, right? Just some creepy woods. Nothing to it. And you have your phone.

She exhaled and tried to look calm, yet she couldn't stop her hand from clenching her phone, the app opened and ready to do its thing.

"All right," she mumbled to herself as she passed the dead tree.

I wonder if I should just play the sounds now. That should keep the bears away, right? She thought about it and shook her head as she kept walking. *Maybe that's a bad idea. What if it makes them feel threatened?*

The familiar crumbled grey walls of the village's stone buildings appeared through the lines of trees in the distance. Olivia made sure she checked the path she was on, memorizing the trail and the trees around it. Mihai and Elena weren't that far, but she still wanted to have a quick way out just in case. Suddenly her foot kicked against a tin can. She looked down. Another cat-food can. *This was the spot!*

Her eyes widened as she recognized a patch of grass and a tree stump up ahead. She ran to it and started her search, bending over and parting grass with her foot to scan for a silver shimmer. Nothing. She sighed and directed her attention to another area when she suddenly heard the snapping of a branch behind her.

She turned around, her phone shaking in her hand. But it was just Mihai standing behind her.

"Oh, thank God, it's just you." She smiled nervously. "For a moment I thought it was another bear."

She didn't notice the hand hidden behind him until he brought it out and took a quick step toward her. A rush of adrenaline shot through her veins—the cold tingle of fear. But it was too late. The last thing she saw was the rock as he struck her with it—a heavy grunt, a loud thud, and everything went black.

***

The van had barely stopped moving when Christian jumped out of it. He pushed through the gate and stormed across the courtyard and into the entrance hall of the castle.

"Olivia!"

Nothing.

He glanced around, fuming, then heard Alina's cries from the library. He found her sitting on a couch next to the fireplace, crying. He ran up to her and grabbed her arms. She looked up at him, sniffling and wiping her tear-stained, swollen face.

"Where is she?" he yelled at Alina, but she continued sobbing, her lips open as if she were trying to speak.

"Alina, look at me!" he said and shook her. "Where is Olivia!"

"I'm ... so sorry," she managed to mutter as more tears flowed down her cheeks. "I told them not to ..." She sniffled. "She promised not to hurt her."

"Where are they? Where did they take her?" his voice resonated through the hall.

"She said they were taking her to the well to scare her. She said they wouldn't hurt her. Just ... just a scare. But I'm worried they'll hurt her."

Christian let go of Alina and turned around to bolt down the hall as fast as he could, leaping down the steps as if he had wings.

I'm coming, Olivia.

***

The darkness faded slowly and with it came the dull pain and the smell of fresh dirt and grass. At first it seemed so far away, the pain, but it spread and jolted her fully awake. Olivia groaned softly and opened her eyes, blinking slowly. Her head throbbed and everything around her was blurry.

Something cold and hard poked into her back, and she felt cold wetness of the grass under her legs. She was sitting on the ground, leaning against a wall of sorts. Slowly, the woods came into a blurry focus, then the wall of the well behind her. Her legs were almost completely submerged in high, wet grass. She winced as the pain in her head sharpened. Even though her mind was cloudy, she knew she was in that old village.

"What ... what happened?" she mumbled and touched the top of her head, where the pain radiated. She winced and withdrew her hand to look at it—bright red blood, lots of it.

She tried to remember what happened when she noticed movement in the corners of her eyes and felt hands grasping her arms from both sides. The voices rose around her. Familiar voices. She was not alone! Elena and Mihai were right next to her, griping her so tightly it hurt.

"You did not hit her hard enough!" Elena growled.

"Just shut up and help me push her in," he barked.

Olivia's eyes shot wide open in terror as her vision become crystal clear and she realized what they were about to do. The well was right next to her, and the two struggled to lift her off the ground, holding her arms and legs.

She let out a wild screamed and started kicking like a wild animal, fighting them with all her might. Yet it seemed pointless; she was weak, and Mihai had a good grip on her.

"Help!" she yelled. "Help!"

"Shut up!" Elena hissed.

Olivia felt her body lift off the ground. "Help!" She tried to kick harder and free her legs. When she saw an arm poke out from underneath her shoulder, she twisted sideways and bit the exposed limb as hard as she could. The metallic flavor of blood filled her mouth as Mihai let out a loud scream.

"Bitch!" he shouted and punched her in the face. The pain was terrible. She felt her lip split open as more blood poured into her mouth.

"Help me!" Olivia cried out again, her voice desperate and filled with rage. A few moments later she felt the hard, cold rock surface of the well on her back as Elena and Mihai heaved her onto the well's wall. Her torso was dangling over the edge now! She jerked her gaze, stared down into the stretching darkness of the well, and screamed.

"Help! Help me! Please help!" She continued kicking and scream-ing and wriggling against their grasps as they pushed her farther and farther over the edge of the well. Olivia was desperate; she was about to die. *Mom, save me,* she prayed just as Mihai let out a loud, pain-filled cry.

His iron grip on her arms loosened and, almost immediately, Elena's too. Olivia let out a grunt as her body thudded backward against the wet floor, her head barely missing a sharp rock sticking out of the ground.

Stretching her trembling hand against the well, Olivia pushed against the rocky wall and rolled away from it through the grass. Breathing hard, she lifted herself onto her knees and saw Christian wrestling with Mihai over the rifle he always carried over his shoulder a few feet ahead of her. Behind them, she saw Elena fleeing into the woods.

Christian let go of the rifle to land a solid punch, which made Mihai drop it and stumble backward, but the moment Christian tried to grab it, Mihai managed to launch onto him and wrap an arm around Christian's neck. Squeezing tightly, he started dragging him toward the well. Olivia jumped to her feet and eyed the rifle in the grass, but Christian was too close to Mihai. And she didn't know how to shoot, anyway. The world spun as she grabbed the rock her head had almost landed on and tumbled toward Mihai, who had pushed Christian against the well, his arm still firmly wrapped around Chris-tian's neck.

"No!" Olivia screamed as Mihai used his free arm to lift Christian's torso sideways over the edge of the well. Christian held on to the stone wall, one of his legs already dangling inside. Mihai hammered his fist onto Christian's hands as they gripped the edge. Olivia launched for-ward, slamming the rock into the back of Mihai's head. The big man stumbled backward and yelled out in pain. Then he straightened and turned toward Olivia.

"You American bitch!" he yelled. His face contorted in anger as he leaped toward her. Suddenly, the loud thunder of a rifle shot ripped through the air. Olivia and Mihai both turned to find Christian aiming at Mihai.

Mihai spat on the ground. "What you gonna do, boy, shoot me?"

With the rifle aimed at Mihai, Christian walked slowly over to Olivia. "I will if I have to, so don't make me."

Mihai laughed, his back facing the well. "I don't believe you," he said, stepping forward.

Christian adjusted the gun against his shoulder. "Step back!" he yelled.

But Mihai took another step forward, and another.

Christian pulled the trigger and another loud shot exploded through the woods. Olivia covered her mouth with her hands in horror as she watched Mihai slowly stumble backward, all the way against the well. His eyes were wide in fear as he lost his balance and fell backward down the well. His screams echoed for a moment before suddenly silenced by a distant thud.

"Christian!" Olivia shouted and threw herself into his arms. He gasped and dropped the rifle into the grass, breathing hard. She hugged him, burying her face in his chest as she sobbed. He held her close.

"You saved my life."

"I guess that makes us even," he responded, kissing her head.

CHAPTER SIXTEEN

I t was already getting dark when the gloved hands of the young male paramedic carefully moved along Olivia's head in the back of the ambulance. The pain at the back of her head had somewhat subsided at this point. A paramedic offered her an injection for the pain, but she'd declined, taking off her bloody, dirt-covered jacket.

Olivia looked in awe at the police cars parked around the castle, the blue lights flashing across its towering, dark walls. It had been a mad rush soon after they called for help and the police and ambulances finally drove in, with uniformed people jumping out and moving around like busy ants. Voices crackled over radios, people spoke loud in the local dialect, and sirens blared.

"Wow," she muttered to herself as the paramedic finally let go of her head. "What a vacation."

"Your head is fine. You just need rest," the paramedic informed her, speaking slowly in a thick accent. "We can still take to hospital for the night, to watch you."

"That's all right. I think I'm okay," she said. The man nodded and left.

"My Lady," someone called out and she smiled without having to look up. Christian strode over to the ambulance. He had a bandage wrapped around his right arm where the bear had wounded him. His hair was wild and his white shirt was stained with blood and mud.

"How are you feeling?" he asked.

Olivia touched the bandage around her head and shrugged. "I'm not inside a well." She rose and stepped to the edge of the ambulance. Christian helped her down from the ambulance, taking her hand in his.

"Me neither."

They both smiled in relief, sharing that subtle dread that came with the realization that either of them could have died.

"This has been one crazy day." Olivia rested her head on his shoulder, watching the police come in and out of the castle and getting search dogs out of their cars, most likely to find Elena.

"And one hell of a tour," Christian said.

Another police car pulled up and the door opened and Christian's mother rushed out. Olivia recognized her instantly, and thinking about it now, she understood how she'd mistaken her for his wife. Christian's mother was a beauty, even with the mix of worry and relief on her face as she limped toward them with a cane.

Olivia stepped away to give her room to embrace her son, crying and squeezing him as if trying to make sure he was real.

Still crying, she said something in Romanian, then turned to Olivia. A bright smile filled her face. There was something else in her eyes that Olivia couldn't quite place. A sort of familiarity she didn't understand.

She leaned forward and hugged Olivia too. "Thank God you are okay," she said softly in a thick Romanian accent. "Maria must be watching over you."

Olivia's mother's name on this woman's lips was disorienting. Olivia stared at her in confusion, wanting to ask if she'd known her mother, when the sound of barking dogs and yelling officers distracted her.

"They found her," Christian translated the hollers for Olivia as a group of officers, all dressed in dark blue, came out of the woods. A German shepherd with a harness that had the words *K-9* written on it was leading the way. Shortly after, two more officers appeared from the thick brush of the forest. They held Elena by the arms, her hands in handcuffs. She kept trying to shrug away from the officers, muttering what Olivia assumed was a string of curses. Olivia couldn't help but feel betrayed; all those nice smiles and tender words were nothing but despicable, evil lies.

One of the officers, a young, skinny guy who looked barely eighteen, announced something and jabbed a finger back toward the forest.

"I think it's about to get crazier," Christian said, gritting his teeth, his eyes hard when he looked at her. "They said they need a medic team at the well. Mihai is still alive."

Olivia sighed, relief and anger flowing through her veins. "That's good. I don't want him to die."

Elena grunted and spat again, her eyes flashing like a caged animal. Her hair stuck out in all directions, covered in dirt and leaves. Her clothes were dirty and torn, like she'd been rolling around in the dirt for hours.

Olivia kept her gaze on her and when their eyes met, Elena threw her a hateful glance. Christian's mother stepped toward Elena, gripping her cane so tight, her white knuckles shook around it.

"How could you, Elena!" she shouted in English, a look of raw disgust on her face as she walked a few more steps toward Elena. The officers ignored her and ushered Elena into one of the many police cars.

"To your own blood!" Christian's mother shouted right before the young, skinny officer pushed Elena's head down to get her into the back of the car. The words rang through the air as Elena's mud-smeared face morphed into a look of shock.

Olivia turned toward Christian's mother. "What did you just say?"

Christian's mother turned to face her, both brows raised high.

"You said, 'to your own blood.' What . . . what did you mean by that?" Olivia asked, stepping closer, Christian right next to her.

His mother narrowed her eyes for a moment, then sighed. "You didn't know?" she asked Olivia, her gaze once again softening.

"Know what?"

"So Maria and Andrei did make you a daughter of secrets then. I advised both of them against it."

A hard lump formed in Olivia's throat. She walked toward Christian's mother without taking her eyes off her.

"Daughter of secrets? What secrets?"

His mother pinched her lips.

"Mom?" Christian said, and she nodded slowly.

"Elena is your aunt."

The words hit so hard, it was almost as if someone had punched her.

"But . . . that would mean . . ."

Nodding, Christian's mother added, "Andrei Rusu was your father."

Olivia stood paralyzed, her feet rooted to the ground. Christian touched his mother's arm. "Are you sure about this, Mom? I thought they were just distant relatives."

Olivia remained silent, her lips twitching. Her shaking hand instinctively moving to the bare spot on her neck before she remembered that her necklace was gone.

"Andrei is her father," his mother insisted before reaching for Olivia's hand to squeeze it tenderly. "Many years ago, Maria told me that she was pregnant with a girl. She told me the day before she left for America. She . . ." Her voice cracked and she exhaled deeply. "She made me swear to her not to say a word." She exhaled and looked up to the sky. "Forgive me, Maria, for breaking my promise, but it's been so long, and I thought she knew." Then she focused her gaze back on Olivia.

Andrei was my father? My real dad? She'd suspected it at first—a distant notion in her mind. Why else leave her all this money? But Mr. Stanley had made it clear to her that Andrei was not her father.

Olivia lowered her gaze, her eyes filling with burning tears. "But why did they lie to me?" she finally spoke, still frozen on the spot. "Why did neither of them say anything to me? And what about my dad? I mean, not Andrei . . . but . . . my dad. Did he know?"

Christian's mother took her in her arms, speaking tenderly. "Your mother loved you madly even before you were born. She would never keep something from you if it wasn't for the best."

Olivia was still in her arms, ready to unleash an avalanche of questions, when she noticed a few officers leading a crying and handcuffed Alina out of the castle by her arms.

"Wait!" she shouted and broke away from Christian's mother. Wiping her teary eyes, she rushed over to them. "What are you doing?"

The officers exchanged puzzled looks as Alina's eyes grew wide. She stared at Olivia in anticipation. "This has to be a mistake," Olivia explained. "She helped save my life."

Christian joined them, threw Olivia a *really?* look, then rolled his eyes in defeat. "It's true," he said. "She told me where to find them."

The officers nodded and released their harsh, forceful grip around Alina's arms. "She'll still have to come to the station for questioning now."

Alina looked at them and nodded.

The only female officer of the group, a middle-aged, oval-faced woman, turned to Olivia as she uncuffed Alina. "We'll come for your statement in the morning after you've had some rest. Same for you two." The woman glanced at Christian and his mother.

Olivia nodded and faintly smiled at Alina, who rubbed her wrists and stared at the ground, both cheeks flushed with shame.

"I'm so, so sorry, Olivia." Her voice was strained.

"It's okay. I know you didn't know that they wanted to hurt me," Olivia tried to reassure her.

Alina shook her head. "I didn't." She sobbed again. "Please believe me."

"Come," the female officer said and grabbed Alina by her arm, this time less forcefully, "you two can talk tomorrow."

Alina nodded and left with the group of officers, looking at Olivia one more time before entering the female officer's police car—in the front.

One by one, the cars started to pull out of the castle, blue lights flashing and wheels crunching. Olivia, Christian, and his mother watched them drive off.

After they'd gone, Christian turned to Olivia. "Why did you help her? You could have easily let her suffer with her mother."

Olivia smiled. "I don't think she knew. A woman who dreams of becoming a doctor and saving lives makes for a bad killer. And besides, she's the only family I have left. I've always dreamt of a hidden relative here in Romania, and despite a pretty crazy introduction, Alina is just that. Back home, well, whatever that is now, I don't really have anyone."

"You have the Rusu fortune," he joked.

Christian put his hands in his pockets. "I guess you'll return to the U.S. after the police get your statement. Mission accomplished, right?" his voice was heavy.

She smiled faintly, shaking her head. "I need a bit of time to recover . . . maybe some therapy . . . but I think I'll stick it out in Romania a bit longer. Get to know Alina, maybe find some good use for this ol' thing." She threw a nod at the castle. "If there is a tour guide willing to drive me around in his terrible van, that is."

He pulled her in and kissed her. "Don't talk about my van like that. She has been my girl before this American woman showed up."

Olivia stood on her toes and kissed him back, whispering, "Should I be jealous?"

They both laughed and turned to Christian's mother when she cleared her throat, an adoring smile on her face.

Olivia grew serious again. "Will you tell me everything you know about my parents?"

"I'm afraid I don't really know much more than I've already told you," she said. "I know your mother and Andrei were in love since childhood. They got married at a very young age, against his family's wishes, especially Elena's. What could one mad sister do to a marriage, one might think, but Elena is not just a sister. She caused your mother and father pain whenever she could. They never talked about the details of their struggles with Elena openly, not even to me, despite Maria and I being friends since childhood."

Olivia shook her head. "But why would my mother just leave with me? Lie to me?"

"I don't know. It was out of the blue when she left, a shock to the whole town. Your mother came to me that night and told me she was pregnant and that she had plans to live in America. The next day she was gone." She sighed and gazed into the distance as if watching that day play out all over again.

"Your mother made me promise never to say a word to anybody about it. I think your parents divorced shortly after. From there, Andrei became richer and richer with this food chain he built from the ground. That's all I know."

Olivia felt the cold tingle of disappointment in her stomach. She tried to hide it with a smile.

Christian and his mother exchanged glances.

"Tell me," his mother asked, "does the kitchen in this old place work?"

Olivia nodded.

"Then come now, let's calm our nerves with a cup of my famous Turkish coffee."

"You're going to love this," Christian whispered and held her close. "It has tsuika in it."

"Tsuika?"

"Liquor."

"Uh-oh." Despite having lived through the worst day of her life, and having her family history turned on its head, Olivia felt a warm glow of happiness radiate through her. Finally, after all these years, she had people around her who cared for her, and wanted her to be happy. It was a new feeling. No, not new. It was a lost feeling she had longed for since she had found herself all alone. She'd yearned for this more than all the money in the world.

Christian led the way up the stairs, followed by Olivia, who held his mother's arm and helped her conquer the enormous stone steps up to the castle. As soon as he stepped through the gigantic wooden doorway, a black crow flew out, trailed by loud caws that echoed through the air. He gasped aloud, and Olivia threw back her head in laughter.

"Can we go back to my house tomorrow?"

"What?" Olivia said. "Come on. I'm actually starting to like this place."

Christian sighed.

"At least let us have it cleansed by the church," his mother suggested.

"We can arrange for that," Olivia said and smiled at Christian, who rolled his eyes.

"I think I remember where the kitchen was," his mother said and entered the castle. Olivia was about to follow her when Christian grabbed her hand and pulled her back. His beautiful brown eyes were bright as he kissed her once more, pressing her closer to him. He gently caressed her chin after breaking the kiss.

"I'm glad you're starting to like this place, because I won't let you leave again soon," he whispered before joining his mother inside. Olivia's heart felt light and free. And when she stepped inside the castle, for this first time, she felt as if this was just the beginning of her life here in Romania . . . with the family she had always longed for.

EPILOGUE

The following summer Elena and Mihai were still in prison. Unlike Mihai, who would spend the rest of his life behind bars, Elena was going to be sent to a guarded retirement home. Turned out, her health actually did decline quickly in prison. Karma was paying her back. Olivia had arranged this transfer with the best lawyer in Romania—and a few generous donations to local politicians.

Olivia looked at herself in the dark wooden mirror that leaned against the wall of her bedroom. It was the same room she first stayed at in the castle when she arrived all those months ago. She had made it her room—hers and Christian's, that is.

"I think it's better this way. Alina has suffered enough after losing her mother like this," Olivia said to Christian as she put her brown curls into a bun. She straightened her flower-patterned, white summer dress and tapped her necklace, which had been returned to her after the court proceedings were over. "I know what it's like to lose a mother. I think the retirement home will be better."

Christian came up from behind and wrapped his muscular arms round her waist. His handsome reflection appeared in the mirror over her shoulder. He looked stunning, as always.   "I wish I could tell you not to do it. But then, your kind heart is the very reason I love you." He kissed her cheek.

The Magura Castle was changing. They all lived there now—Olivia, Christian, his mother and sisters, and Alina. Together, they were turning it into a free boarding school for troubled kids. Alina would soon only be able to help during semester breaks, since her university dreams had already been set in motion.

Olivia's gaze briefly dropped to the simple, silver engagement ring on her finger before she grinned, as she always did when she looked at it. Christian had proposed about a month ago. He had apologized that it was all he could afford, and she called him silly to apologize for that and started bawling in happiness as she said, "Yes!" Next to her necklace, it was the most beautiful thing she possessed.

"It's funny how much less grey this place seems now," she said.

"It's the endless noise from my sisters. And soon there will be even more," he said. "Maybe even . . ." he added, placing his hand on her belly.

"I told you, I'd let you know as soon as it happens." Olivia laughed. "No need to ask me twice a day!"

"All right, how about once then?"

She smacked his shoulder and freed herself from his embrace. "Are the girls back from school yet?"

A loud drilling noise echoed though the hallway into the room. The castle had been full of noise lately—construction sounds, laughter, and vehicles coming in and out.

"There! They're over there!" Ana's high-pitched voice thundered though the hallway. She was followed by the rest of the gang: Daria, Sofia, and Gabriela, who were, in turn, followed by Christian's mother, who used the newly installed elevators over the endless stairs.

Ana was waving a white envelope as she ran. Olivia could never get enough of them—these precious little girls, always jumping or singing, their voices filled with life and happiness.

"You have a letter," Sofia hollered and snatched the letter out of Ana's hand. They were all dressed in pink summer dresses, school backpacks still strapped over their shoulders, their golden hair shimmering in the rays of light coming in from the window.

"Hey!" Ana stomped her foot. "I wanted to give it to Olivia!"

Sofia grinned. She was a head smaller than Ana, yet she was running the show. Handing it over to Olivia, Sofia grinned when Olivia gave her ponytail a playful tug.

"Thank you, Princess Sofia," Olivia said, and the little girl raised her chin briefly before they all thundered back out into the hallway, high-pitched screams surrounding them as the chased one another.

Olivia looked down at the letter in her hands. It had Mr. Stanley's Boston address on it.

"It's from Mr. Stanley, my lawyer. Strange," Olivia said with a puzzled look on her face as she opened it. Inside the envelope was a letter and another envelope, one smaller and somewhat older looking. Olivia held the first letter closer to her face and read in silence.

Dear Ms. Olivia "Rusu,"

I trust you've received the letters. There isn't much to say except a simple apology. I knew Andrei and his sister had issues, but I had absolutely no knowledge of her true evil nature; otherwise I would have never let you get on that plane. I wonder if Andrei truly knew who she really was...

In any case, I have something for you. The other letter attached to this one is from Andrei Rusu, your father. I'm sorry I could not hand it to you earlier. Under attorney-client privilege, Andrei had strictly instructed that this letter should never be handed to you unless you somehow discovered the truth about who you really are. There were times I came close to telling you, but then, Andrei was more than my client. He was my friend, and I owed it to him to keep my word.

Forgive me. May you he and you be at peace at last.
Marcus Stanley

Olivia hesitated, her heart beating fast. She flipped over the other envelop, no inscriptions, nothing. Taking a deep breath, she tore open the top, slipping out the letter. The handwriting was familiar—she'd seen it on some of the books in the library.

Feeling Christian's warm hand on her shoulder, she braced herself and read.

My dear daughter,

If you are reading this letter, it means that you have come to Romania to share your fortune with my undeserving sister and are as kindhearted as your mother was. But it also means that you have found out the truth and that you have met your aunt Elena. I can only hope that she is not giving you any grief. The death of our parents and being forced to raise me in poverty when she herself was only a child changed her forever. It made her heart cold, her mind greedy and clouded. In my heart, I blame her for the love of my life leaving me, even though my mind tells me no one but myself is to blame.

I might not be able to provide the peace that you deserve, but I do have the answers that might someday lead to it.

When your mother and I got married, we were both very young. I was just starting out with a restaurant in a nearby town. It was a great success, and I was able to open two more in Bucharest. After that, I was constantly busy and forced to take trips away from your mother. I was gone when your mother called me, in panic, her voice terrified and desperate. She said that her and Elena had a terrible argument over money, and that she woke up to the house smelling of gas. The firefighters said the stove had leaked gas all night, and that your mother would be dead if she hadn't slept with her window open like she always did. With a heavy heart, I have to tell you that your mother accused Elena of trying to kill her.

To this day, I still can't wrap my head around my sister, but I know for a fact that your aunt Elena is not the kind-hearted and loving person I always wished her to be. If you came to Romania to share the fortune with her, do so and then stay away from her. Knowing what I now know, it was a mistake to doubt your mother. Sweet Maria forgave me those doubts and begged me to sell the restaurants and move far away with her, but, being the young fool that I was, I couldn't. I was becoming more successful by the day, was blinded by the riches that this world had in store for me. I was growing richer and richer, more powerful and important, until one day, Maria was gone.

Here I'm sitting now, writing this letter, looking back, willing to give it all up, the money, the success, the power, just to be with you and your mother again.

It didn't take me a whole lifetime to realize what I'd lost, but when this old fool finally saw clearly again, it was already too late. Your mother had remarried, a good man, a man who would call himself your father and act the part as well.

The first time I watched you from the distance coming out of the school, holding your mother's hand, I knew you were mine. Your hair, your eyes, your smile. You were a Rusu. You had the same strength in your eyes. And yet, you were not mine to claim. What kind of man would I be to destroy what she'd built for the two of you?

The only gift I could give you was to leave you be . . . and leave alone the memory of your mother and American father—the man you had always known as your dad, the one who was there when you blew out the candles on your first birthday cake, the man who held you when you cried over your first broken heart.

And that was not me. I was the bad guy in this drama, the man who reached for the stars, and ended up with full pockets and an empty heart.

Please don't to be mad at your mother. She did the right thing.
For what it is worth, I love you.
Please forgive an old fool.

Love, Andrei—Dad

Christian had been standing by her the whole time, staring at her in anticipation as she read the letters. He let her have the moment, but held her in his arms when her face flushed and the tears started to stream down her cheeks. He wiped her face with his hand as she looked up at him.

"I finally know who I really am."

She ripped out the last part of the letter, which said *Love, Andrei—Dad*, and took out her necklace, placing the slip of paper into the locket with the picture of her parents. It felt amazing, as if she were finally complete, like a broken piece of a vase, forgotten for years, glued back on.

They heard the thudding of feet and the playful laughter of Christian's sisters, who'd been playing hide and seek in the hallway—behind the statues of knights. Suddenly, one of the helmets of one of the metal knight statues fell off, banging against the floor with an echoing metallic sound before rolling down the hallways a few feet and coming to a halt right in front the wide-open bedroom door. The knight now looked beheaded, robbed of all its honor and glory. All four of the girls took one look at the headless knight and bolted.

"Hey! Come back here!" Christian yelled after them as his mom hobbled after them. Olivia burst into laughter.

"That's not funny, Olivia! Last week they knocked a deer's head off the wall after they decided to throw rocks at it."

"Because it scared them," Olivia said with a smile. "It was a little scary . . . and ugly."

"Maybe so, but—"

"Besides," Olivia said, "we usually get an hour alone after they get in trouble." She placed her palm on his stomach

"When you put it that way, I hope they tear this place apart," he said, closing the door and locking it. He swept her off her feet. She laughed as her cheeks turned red. This was the happiness she'd craved, the family she'd longed to be a part of, and now she had it all.

THE END

OUR RECOMMENDATION!

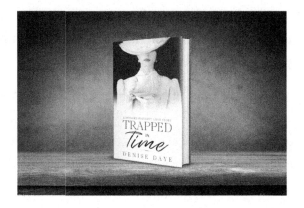

After an accident, Emma Washington wakes up in Victorian England — and in order to survive, she must do the one thing she's been avoiding her whole life: get married. But what if her betrothal to notorious Lord William Blackwell leads to true love?

The book is available on Amazon: (FREE with Kindle Unlimited)

https://www.amazon.com/dp/B083N237V9

THANK YOU!

First of all, thank you for purchasing Daughter of Secrets. I know you could have picked any number of books to read, but you picked this book, and for that I am extremely grateful. As a small-time author and full-time mom, my readers mean the world to me!

If you enjoyed this book, it would be really nice if you could leave a review for it on Amazon.

You can review the book here:

https://www.amazon.com/dp/B08NYWTS6H

Your feedback and support will help me to continue writing romance novels.

Also, don't forget to sign up for our newsletter to stay up to date on new releases and get FREE novels. You can find the newsletter and more info about our books here:

www.timelesspapers.com

Thank you!

ABOUT THE AUTHOR

Denise graduated with a Master's in Social Work from an Ivy League school and has spent many years of her life supporting families and individuals in need of assistance. She has always had a passion for writing, but it wasn't until her own baby boy was born that Denise turned her passion into her profession. Whenever Denise is not typing away on one of her books, you can find her caring for her son (aka one of the toughest jobs in the world), binging Netflix with her beloved husband, or chasing after her puppy (who should technically be an adult dog by now).

Made in the USA
Monee, IL
09 July 2021